Dim Tales

Dim Tales

John Knoepfle

Stormline Press
Urbana, Illinois
1989

International Standard Book Number: 0-935153-12-8

Library of Congress Number: 89-061575

Stormline Press, Inc., a non-profit service organization, publishes works of literary and artistic distinction. The press is particularly interested in those works which accurately and sensitively reflect rural and small town life.

Stormline Press, Inc.
P.O. Box 593
Urbana, Illinois 61801

Manufactured in the United States of America.

Publication of this book is made possible in part by a grant from the Illinois Arts Council, a state agency.

The Dim stories were originally made up for the telling. I wish to thank all those who listened to them in the middle '80s when most of them were composed. Thanks also, to Bill Rintz, who recorded many of them for his program, "Folk Festival" on WSSR, now WSSU. My thanks to Gary DeNeal, who has been publishing the stories as I have been able to transcribe them in his *Springhouse: A Journal of the Illinois Ozarks,* and to Kevin Stein, editor of the *Illinois Writers Review,* who published "The Hannibal Frogs" in the spring 1988 issue. I owe a debt of gratitude to Springfield writer Debi Edmund, who transcribed my bad script onto a disk. And especially to my editor Peggy Knoepfle, who kept me from straying too far from the spoken word, which is where these stories began. The text for Dim's favorite poem, "When the Dim Day," can be found in *The Complete Poems of Frederick Goddard Tuckerman.* Words in "Dim's dream" were derived from Lincoln's "Fairwell to Springfield."

A note concerning Dim

Everything about Dim is a little obscure. His family is supposed to have come from Maine, but this is based on the single report that his mother once paddled him in a canoe. Whatever, he used to sit with the other old-timers in back of the pharmacy. He liked to hold his cup of coffee in the palms of his hands, his elbows propped on the table, so that he could blow steam from the coffee across the cup while he would be thinking of something interesting to say.

Henry Allison Rollins Dim was his full name, but he was called Hardy locally. He is probably best known throughout central Illinois—and the world, too, in some ways—for his wise sayings, most of which were concocted while he was jawing with his friends on weekday mornings. The pharmacy was closed on Sundays. Most people have heard, for instance, of "The man who holds the basket the longest catches the leaf." Or how about, "The nibbled hotdog is not a good loser"? Dim had the genius for summing up a thing so well in a given situation that there was nothing left to say about it: for example, "The woman who has no money in her purse may have had some at one time; on the other hand, it may be that she never did have any." I think everyone recognizes "Suck an egg today, scramble one tomorrow" as the very quintessence of Dim. But there are many others, such as "It always rains in rectangles on a deck full of aces," and "The flea on the elevator will take a giant step for mankind."

Dim died, as he had lived, sad to say or not depending on how you feel about proverbs, by his word. One time his friends were talking in old moans about the cost of everything going up. Dim sat there, elbows on the table, pooching little ripples over the surface of his coffee. Then he said, "In a time of inflation the camel. . . ." The others waited for him to finish, but he just sat there until one of his friends said, "I think this is all for Dim," and took the cup from his hands and put it on the table. Dim was just sitting there deceased, holding on to his last maxim, as people described it later.

My interest in Dim was stimulated when I bought blind a carton of stuff at a garage sale in Zenobia, Illinois. Zenobia is south of 104 a little over on the east side of Pawnee, well a number of miles in truth, and not far from the power plant. It turned out that this box had a lot of things in it that had traveled from garage sale to garage sale. There was a centennial napkin from New Berlin, for instance, and plastic forks and spoons that were marked "Courtesy of the State Bank of Rolling Meadows," all pretty much junk unless you were in the business of collecting commemorative napkins and plastic tableware. But at the very bottom of the box, down there flat, were a number of dog-chewed spiral notebooks. I discovered when I got the box home that the notebooks were filled with scribblings and small sketches by Dim. His initials were always in the upper left corner of the cover when you opened one of the spiral books.

During the years since, as time would allow, I have pieced Dim's stories together, reconstituting them from their often dismembered state in the notebooks. Now that they are being brought to press, I hope that this facet of Dim's talent for shaping the experiences of his life into stories will be as appreciated as his ability to draw proverbs from the common knowledge of mankind.

John Knoepfle
March 31, 1989

Dim names the strangers

This is the story of some strange people who came into town and they were all driving old Volkswagen buses, all crammed with folks. They looked reasonably like other people, but their volume and emphasis, the way they put their words down, wasn't quite right. They'd say things like, "How you doing?" which everybody can say in central Illinois, you know, but they put the stress on the "how" and not on the "doing," so people felt they were aliens or something. Perhaps they were travelers from outer space or as one old fellow said, they might have been gypsies. There's a history of gypsies in this area. Or then again they could have been the remnant of some native American group that never left Illinois.

Anyway, several old men got out of the buses and went into the police station, they were friendly enough, but they had this strange request. They said they were passing through and they were dissatisfied with their names and wanted somebody in town to suggest new names for them. The various policemen scratched their heads and talked back and forth about this. Then one of them suggested that Dim was into reading, so he was the one they should talk to.

Well, they all drove over to Dim's house. He was flattered that they would want to come to him and since he had just made a trip from Cincinnati back west into the middle of Illinois, what he did was he gave each of the old men, because each one was a clan leader of some importance, a name that he'd picked up on the highway. He named one Next Right and then there was one he called Harrison Bowl and there was Exit and Slow and Merge, names like that, like Minimum.

They thanked him and as it turned out they were like the Swiss who came into Highland, they came with resources and just bought land and settled down. And so what they did was they bought a lot of land in that wild country over near Fishhook, which is about halfway between Quincy and Meredosia on the other side of the Illinois River. And you know, Dim later said it proved things out. If you have in this country a name with two words in it and a hyphen, you've got a leg up on prosperity. The Harrison-Bowls became very prominent and rather conservative citizens over there and the Next-Rights were successful politicians. They were senators and judges. Judge Next-Right was famous for some of his decisions. He wrote a book on torts that became a required text in India.

But the Slows didn't do too well and they should never have intermarried with the Merges. That was a social disaster. There were Slow Merges all over western Illinois. Everybody liked the Minimums. They were invited to all the church socials and family reunions. They were good singalong people. As for the Exits, no one ever knew what happened to them. They just disappeared somewhere.

Dim kept in touch with those people. They'd send him little postcards and scrawls on the backs of their envelopes, and things like that. So that's the story of how Dim named the strangers.

Dim and Louie de Flees

Now it was that time of year when it suddenly begins to get very cold and as if by magic these multicolored lights appear in the windows of the houses and wrapped around evergreen trees in the yards, you know, pretty lights, yellows and blues and reds and greens, and the big star, illuminated star, appears on the grain elevator just this side of the railroad tracks near the town square. Well, one night at this time Dim's dog Sleuth was out. You may not have heard how Sleuth engaged in the great chase of I-Ching, chased the rabbit around the world, but he was a much older dog now, and indeed Sleuth's idea of a fine afternoon was just to go out and have a good bark.

Anyway, he was out this night and there was a soft feathery snow sparkling on the sidewalks and he was sniffing and dancing his way along in the evening when he came to an alley. There was a trash can there and he heard inside the trash can this pitiful whining. Sleuth understood that one of his kind was in the trash can and he would have turned it over except that it was chained to the ground. So he went back at a kind of loping gallop to his house and stood at the door and barked at Dim, tried to encourage him to come out. Then he pulled on Dim's pants leg until Dim figured, well, Sleuth wanted him to go walking in the snow. Sleuth led him to the trash can and Dim too heard the little whining sound, so he reached in there and he cupped his hands around a small ball of shivering excitement. Well, of course, it was a little puppy. Dim took it back, you couldn't leave it there, you know, and Dim had a soft heart. So he took the little animal back and it was pretty dirty and it was quite late that night, so he just put him down on a pile of old rugs near the furnace in the basement and gave him some warm milk, and the little dog was so grateful to be there that he didn't whine or anything all night long, just stayed down there and rested.

Well, the next day Dim brought him up and put him in the bathroom sink and washed him off, took all the bugs off, and that's when he understood that this was a French dog and that his name was Louie de Flees. It was all very nice at first. The little dog liked to sleep on the heater or else he liked to sleep between Sleuth's paws, but as soon as he gained strength, you see, he became like any other puppy and wanted to chew up everything in sight. He chewed a hole in Dim's Turkish rug, for instance. The rug was a factory-made rug, but Dim was kind of sentimental about it. It had been in the family a long time. And Louie chewed the rungs of the chairs and he chewed up slippers and he had some genius for getting ahold of Dim's glasses and chewing the arms off of them. It didn't matter where Dim left his glasses, this little puppy could get up and get at them. And then as he became more vigorous he wanted to play all the time, but poor old Sleuth was beyond jumping around in the kitchen for no particular reason. So Dim understood after a while that he would have to get rid of Louie de Flees. Only he didn't know how to do it, didn't know should he advertise in the paper or what?

The solution was really remarkable. One Saturday morning he took Louie to a flea market and he walked along looking at the exhibits that people were showing there for sale and trade, and Louie was following behind him. At a certain point he came to where there was a mother and father and several little girls, and these little girls said, " *Oh, regardez le bon petit canish!*" Louie knew exactly what they were saying—"Oh, look at that nice little poodle!"—and, you know, he went right over to those little girls and sat down and spoke to them in his best French.

He said, "onn! onn! onn!" like that. Well, the parents of the girls knew that they had been had. So they traded six plastic green glasses for Louie de Flees, and Dim had found Louie a nice home.

Sometimes it would happen in the evenings when he and Sleuth were blinking sleepily in the living room of Dim's house, Dim would think, "Maybe we should have kept Louie." But then he'd say, "Well, those little girls must be giving him a happy home." And then he'd say, "And I got an awfully good swap with those six plastic glasses." Indeed he did, he used them for three or four years before they finally broke. So that's the story of Louie de Flees.

The Lake Springfield monster

I guess you didn't hear about Dim's ice fishing on Lake Springfield? Well, there was a friend of Dim's, this fellow was named Chesmerski. Chortles Chesmerski, he was Lithuanian, one of the miners there south of town. Well, Chortles had to retire early as a miner, he got that name because of his shattering, booming laugh. The other miners were always afraid that something would strike him funny when he was down in the mine and he'd laugh like that and they'd have the roof cave in. So he had to leave early, but he, you know, rather than have some labor dispute, because he was a good miner, the company gave him a nice pension and he never did anything after that except fish. And after that they just called him Ches because they weren't afraid of him laughing anymore.

It was in January and you know it hadn't been above freezing for four weeks when Ches met Dim and said, "Hey Dim, why don't we get some hatchets and go to Lake Springfield near that I-55 bridge and do some ice fishing? Maybe get some of those 20-pound catfish." Well, Dim thought that it was a kind of a wonderful idea, so he and Ches loaded up the car with everything they needed and they went out on the ice there and put this hole through the ice. They didn't build, you know, a house over the hole, a shack, because it was a reasonable day, it was up to about 15 degrees and there was no wind. So it wasn't as if they were ice fishing in Minnesota.

They were just standing there, watching the traffic on the bridge and enjoying the sight of the houses along the lake shore and what they didn't notice was—you know there are stories about Lake Springfield, there's the story about the motorcyclist who somehow jumped the railing along the I-55 bridge and went right into the lake, disappeared, and they sent, the municipal authorities, they sent a professional diver down, you know, and he wasn't down there but a few minutes when he signalled to come back up and when they got him out and got his suit off and everything, his face was ashen and he said he would never go down there again—well, nobody really knows what he saw, he wasn't articulate about that.

But to get back to Dim and Ches, ah, while they were admiring the shoreline, this sucker rose from the bottom of the lake and clamped his round mouth onto the underside of that hole in the ice. Perhaps he was trying to get a little fresh air, who knows? But there he was and Ches and Dim didn't notice.

Well, then Ches took some good fishing line, I don't know what weight it was. It was, it was strong enough so that you could hook a muskellunge. I don't know what he was thinking he'd catch, there aren't any muskies in Lake Springfield. Dim thought Ches's line was overkill, but he didn't want to make an issue about it. Anyway, Ches attached a hook and a doughball and put a weight on there and he dropped it into the hole in the ice. But, you see, what he dropped it into was the gullet of the big sucker. Ches had taken a turn around his wrist with the line, he was just standing there holding the line up above the hole—see, for ice fishing you don't need a pole—well, perhaps in Minnesota, but this was central Illinois. In any case, this sucker swallowed lightly and suddenly Ches was pulled, his arm was all the way down into that hole, all the way up to his shoulder. Dim didn't know what had happened, but he grabbed and he pulled, you know, he pulled at Ches's coat.

Just at that time a truck driver was crossing the bridge with a flatbed truck. He saw Ches and Dim struggling and jammed on his brakes right in the middle of the bridge there. He threw down three or four posts, trying to get one to land close enough to Dim so that Dim could grab it and slide it over the top of the hole, but Dim had a hard time doing that. Well, anyway, while all this was going on and Dim was getting the—I guess it was a four by four, across the hole, the sucker belched slightly and up came Ches, but you see the line was frozen to his hand now. He couldn't let go of it.

Oh, it was terrible and, well, the catfish—did I say catfish? It was a big sucker, it wasn't a catfish at all, it was a sucker. If it had been a catfish, this would have been a different story altogether, but this is one of those sucker stories. Well, more and more people were gathering on the bridge to see what was going on and even with the post across the hole, as soon as the sucker swallowed again, down went Ches with Dim holding onto him. By this time two state troopers had come out on the ice and other truckers had stopped and various car passengers, and they were all out on the bridge.

One of the truckers had a pair of good nylon lines, I guess about an inch, these lines, an inch and a half, they were very strong. So he let them down and the troopers tied the lines to the four-by-four post that Dim had managed to wrap his arm around while still keeping a good grip on Ches. Then the truckers pulled those two lines tight, sort of at angles, you know what I mean? The I-55 bridge has a concrete rail that is surmounted by a tubular steel rail with supports, oh, maybe every five feet. Well, they took the left-hand line and they pulled it through one of the supports and then back out and around the other, they made an "S" figure, you see, for the purchase—so that they could check the line easier. Then they did the same thing with the right-hand line on the other side, so they had a kind of "V" coming up from the hole in the ice. Then they put about 20 people on each of those lines up on the bridge, plus a Freightliner and the flatbed pulling opposite each other.

But, you know, the strain hardly bothered that sucker at all. It just swallowed lightly and down went Ches and Dim. It was a standoff. The people all had their heels dug into the concrete, holding on, and the truck tires were smoking. Then a helicopter came, one of those big army helicopters, and it let down a line directly above Dim and Ches, and the policeman hooked that line around the post and everybody heaved and the helicopter pulled with all of its prop strength up, straight up, and that lifted Ches out of the hole, and Dim too, and everybody cheered. But it was premature because at this point the sucker began to take the contest seriously and he began to inhale and the people who had dug their heels in, it took them straight back across the bridge, their heels grinding all the way right up to the rail, and the trucks were headlight to headlight and the helicopter was straining and coughing blob-blobblobblob up in the air, flapping like a dying swan. And everybody began to say, "Oh oh oh" because you know what was happening? The ice was being pulled down under the whole surface of the lake and the lines were bending the guard rails and the concrete bridge was cracking. The whole world was going down, the sucker was pulling everything down. It was horrible.

It would have been the end of Dim, and Ches too, no question about that. But, you know, just when Ches should have been done for, the whole business of being swallowed by a sucker struck him funny and he let out this laugh that sounded like a superbowl stadium filled with loons. That laugh shook the houses along the shore of the lake and some of the motor boats that were up on davits dropped onto the ice in the boat houses. And the sucker heard the noise and thought it was The Great Loon coming to make a lunch out of him, so he began to think of departing. Dim was alert, too, and he got out his pocket knife, it was really a Swiss silver knife one of his New York uncles had given him. But no matter, he took that knife and cut Ches's muskellunge line and the sucker slowly descended to the bottom of the lake.

So there you have it. Everybody was saved. Of course, it took a while for Ches's arm to thaw out and several days for it to mend and it took almost as long for the people on the bridge to get the ringing out of their ears. As for Ches and Dim, they never went ice fishing again, as you would expect. And miners all over Illinois were glad that Chortles Chesmerski had retired. With a laugh like his, he could have caved in every mine in the state.

The harmonica players of Mount Olive

Here it is the, what is the date? The 24th of January and
you know that it's the birthday of Robert Burns? Didn't you
have haggis and oats? They always eat a bag of oats, the
Scots do on the 24th. Maybe we ought to all sing "Comin
Through the Rye." This reminds me, have you ever been to
Mount Olive down there off Route 55? That's a very interesting town. You know Dim in the days when he was a
traveling salesman happened to be there at one time. He
sold pharmaceutical products, but that has nothing to do
with this story, except that it tells what kind of a salesman
he was. Everybody knew this.

Anyway, one time he happened to be in Mount Olive
and his car broke down and he had to wait in the town
while he was getting a tire fixed up. So Dim was there, but
the townsfolk really thought he had left. If they had
thought he was still there, it never would have happened.
And you know, just at sundown everybody came out and
they all gathered at one particular street intersection and,
well, everybody came except for chronic arthritics and
people with bad legs—everybody else came, and just at
sundown. But I should backtrack a little. There was a
church bell went off with a bong bong bong, like that,

bong bong bong. And they all came out just at sundown, when the church bell rang. That was the signal to come, see. Just at sundown they all came out and stood there and everyone in the town had a harmonica and they all played "Three Blind Mice." Everybody. Old men. Small children. Mothers. They all played "Three Blind Mice." Then when they were finished, they all applauded one another and went home.

Well, Dim was amazed. He wasn't supposed to have seen this. These people didn't like hype. Yes, the reason I believe Dim could tell this story is that they never went out on the same day at the same time. In other words, if you were coming over with your pen and your notebook and camera, they wouldn't be there. But every so often on an unexpected day this church bell bong bong bongs and they all come out at sundown and play "Three Blind Mice." Except whenever they go out on Christmas Eve. Then they play "Jingle Bells." But that isn't very often.

And another thing they do is, and that's what reminds me of it, it's this particular day, they all come out and play "Believe Me if All Those Endearing Young Charms." At least this is what Dim said. This is because none of them knows "Scots! Wha Hae Wi' Wallace Bled" or "John Anderson, My Jo." They have to do a Celtic thing for Bobby Burns, see, and they are all Germans, so, anyway, this is the story of Mount Olive with its proud and particular people who have this little harmonica ritual, probably still going on. At least Dim thought so.

Dim's Chicago epiphany

Well, this is a—Dim recorded this story about going to Chicago in the winter, one time in January. And he was amazed because with a strong head wind up there, people lean into it looking like 10 minutes after two on the clock. And when the wind is behind them, they look like it's 10 of 10. And if they walk into the wind, they have to dig in with their toes and if the wind is behind them, they slide on their heels. But the one constant is that they all make these little cries of pain, they go, "Oh oh oh," like that, in the wind.

And you know, Dim had a revelation. He was astonished, it stood him right straight up in the middle of the Loop like a statue. He suddenly understood that those people crying with such pain are the Chicago Cub fans. So he even, he had a kind of scientific bent of mind—to prove this out he went to a game one summer day at Wrigley Field and sure enough, that's what he found. The fans weren't even watching the game, they were just sitting around going, "Oh oh oh."

So Dim figured that Chicagoans go to Cub games just to keep in condition for the terrible winters. Or maybe, he thought, it's the other way around, he didn't know for sure.

Saved by the Mouse King

Well, this, as Dim recorded it, is a very short story. It seems
that once late at night on Route 104, Dim was set upon by
some thuglike people who stole his wallet and his watch
and valuables and then they tied him up and dumped him
over on the right side of the road, as you're going west,
into Sugar Creek. He ended up caught there on the bank,
he couldn't struggle too much because the creek was
running high and he was afraid he'd slide into it. He was in
a bad way. It was a chilly night and if he'd had to stay
there all night, there is no telling what would have happened to him. He might have died of exposure or slid into
the creek and drowned. But suddenly he heard all these
little cheeping sounds and he looked up in the darkness
and it was the Mouse King coming with all the mice. He
could see the hooped silver of the Mouse King's crown,
shining in the moon's glow. These mice came down the
bank of Sugar Creek and they gnawed the ropes that were
knotted around Dim and he was able to escape.

You might want to know why the mice would do that.
Well, you know, in the country when you get the first cold
snap, the mice all want to come into the house, they want
to have a warm place to spend the winter and people have

to trap them out. Well, Dim always baited his traps with plastic cheese bits. And the mice would gather around the traps and look at that and say, "Well, I think Dim is trying to tell us something" and then they would leave and go somewhere else. So they appreciated his consideration and when he had to have a favor done, they all came and gnawed through the ropes. So that's his story about the generous Mouse King and the mice.

Dim's ring

You remember that Dim traded Louis de Flees for six small
green plastic tumblers? Yes. Well, it was evening of that
same day when Dim was coming back from the fleamarket
and he was beset by four men and dumped over the bridge
at Sugar Creek. And the Mouse King rescued him. But the
men who robbed Dim, they drove quickly to the west, they
passed Waverly on Route 104 and on this side of Jacksonville, between Franklin and Piscah, they came to a roadside
tavern. By then they felt pretty safe, so they wanted to have
some beer and pretzels.

Well, this was like any other little bar, you know,
crowded with people sitting around drinking beer and
there were colored lights revolving behind the bar and
there were games to play, if you were in the mood to play
a game. And the usual people were there, the road graders
were there and the telephone linemen, the farmers and
farm hands and coal miners, and then you're liable to have
the township superintendent of roads sitting there and
maybe the high school principal would be in there, too. It
was Friday night and they were all there.

So, to come back to the four men, they came in and sat
at this table and the neighborhood patrons gave them a

studied eye there for a moment because in these places you mark people that you don't know. But after they'd given them the studied eye, they drifted back to talking again about what spring planting was going to be like and the baseball season coming on, whatever.

Well, these four fellows, after they had a couple of drinks in them, they weren't feeling any pain, eating pretzels and popcorn, peanuts, lots of salt. Where was I? They were sitting there and the fourth man —he was like the other three, but there was a difference. He was wearing a silver ring. And this ring, it was not a store-bought ring. It wasn't handsome or anything, it was crudely done. It must have been a silver coin that some fellow had pounded into the shape of a ring.

Well, that was the same ring Dim had bought earlier in the day at the fleamarket. See, he took a fancy to it, after he traded Louie de Flees for the six plastic tumblers. Dim really was proud of that swap and years later when he'd get one of those tumblers out, he'd tell people about it. He had them, oh, five, six years. But what happened now? To get back to the story, I was led astray by the plastic tumblers.

Anyway, the fourth man was wearing the ring that he had taken from Dim, after Dim had bought it at the flea market. But about those tumblers, Dim had them with him, but they were thrown in the bushes by the thieves. He had gone into the truck stop to get, you know, a piece of pie from one of those microwave ovens, heated up in there, and with a big scoop of vanilla ice cream. But on the way out, and he wasn't about to leave those tumblers in the car because he was afraid—they had a kind of symbolic value always associated with Louie de Flees—well, they jumped him and the tumblers were tossed away. But this fourth man took the silver ring.

But to continue, the bar was crowded. People were gabbing and drinking, talking about the Cubs and the Cards, pennant chances. And the other three men were enjoying the scene. Well, they were having some kind of an argument about whether penicillin was still useful, but nothing came of that. Meantime, the fourth man was sitting there and the ring said to him,
> What is it
> that you know and I know

that nobody else
in this room knows?
A terrible chill went down the spine of the fourth
robber, he couldn't believe what he had heard. And the
ring said again,
What is it
that you know and I know
that nobody else
in this room knows?
Well, he suddenly blurted back to his ring, after thinking seriously for a moment, "We assaulted that man back
there at 104 and 55."
You know, in the early evening when the sparrows are
noising it up in the shrubs and you yell, "Birds, be quiet!"
there's a sudden lull in the twittering and chirping. Well, it
was like that in the bar when the fourth robber said what
he did. There was a lull in the conversation and then the
noise and the chatter in the bar picked up again and even
the other three thieves weren't sure what they had heard.
To go back to the story. As I said, everybody in the bar
was chattering away, talking about mine subsidence and
spring planting, or whatever, and the fourth robber was
sitting like a petrified stump in Arizona, when the ring
asked again,
What is it
that you know and I know
that nobody else
in this room knows?
And the robber stiffened again and he thought and he
thought, and he blurted out, "I stole you off of his finger!"
Suddenly the three other robbers became very alert and
there was that birds-be-quiet lull in the bar, only this time
the birds became a little more quiet and a little more
attentive.
Now what I want to explain is that in that bar that night
everybody was smiling, the home team had won the state
basketball tournament, or something like that. But at the
point when the fourth robber blurted out that he had stolen
the ring, the smiles on the faces of all the people up and
down the bar, those smiles began to fade, and the smiles
on the faces of the three other robbers, those smiles began
to broaden until they were stretched across their faces from
ear to ear as if they had been glued on.

By now the fourth robber didn't care anything about whether the people around him were were smiling or not. His attention was fixed on the ring and he said, "Well, what is the riddle? What is the riddle? Say the riddle again!" And the ring said,
What is it
that you know and I know
that nobody else
in this room knows?
And the fourth robber shouted, "We threw him over the bridge at Sugar Creek."

At this point the other three robbers all began laughing hilariously and saying, "This guy is out of his head, isn't he. He's in his cups, he's drunk as a skunk!" But the people standing around in the bar were facing them now and even their faint half smiles had disappeared. And then those people with no smiles on their faces slowly began to gather around the table where the four robbers were sitting.

And once again the ring spoke to the fourth robber,
What is it
that you know and I know
that nobody else
in this room knows?
There was dead silence in the bar. The three other robbers sat there appalled and all the others standing around them looked expectant. Then the fourth robber blurted out, "The four of us robbed that man up there at I-55 and 104 and then we threw him into Sugar Creek." At that point the circle around the four thieves tightened into a knot.

But I have to tell you something about the ring that I think you will find extremely interesting. There was no writing on this ring or even small decorations, but this ring had been hammered out by a fellow in Africa and, you know, there are places in Africa where there is no stealing. Dim was never able to find out exactly where the ring came from, maybe Chad or Sierra Leone, but wherever it was, the people living there understand that each object has a soul and each soul knows the souls all around it, so if an object, say a water jar, perhaps, is stolen, that water jar knows it has been stolen and it knows the soul of the person who stole it, even if the real owner doesn't know the water jar is gone. Maybe the owner has hundreds of water jars, but that one water jar knows and some terrible thing will happen to the person who took it. The thief's soul will be sick with fear. Maybe an elephant will step on that light-fingered person, who knows? So, it wasn't just a simple-minded ordinary ring that was talking to the fourth robber in the bar that night.

But to return to the story. Various patrons of the bar examined the wallets of the robbers and one of the wallets had the name of Henry Allison Rollins Dim on the driver's license. Well, there were people there who knew Dim. They said, "That's Dim's wallet. They did that to Dim?" And things might have gone badly for those robbers, but an off-duty policeman took charge and carted them to jail. So that's pretty much the story.

Oh, the riddle? When they were in the police car, driving to the jail, the fourth robber said to the ring, "What's the answer? What's the answer?"

And do you know what the ring said? It said,
You knew and I knew
that we were speaking together
but nobody else in that room knew
that we were speaking together.

I can tell you—because Dim corresponded with the fourth robber for several years while that man was serving his time—I can tell you that the fourth robber completely reformed. He never stole another ring as long as he lived.

Tripping over dogs

Dim actually was an entrepreneur before anybody could pronounce the word let alone spell or define it. But he doesn't take full credit for his idea and subsequent involvement in the business community. He was in Chatham one Saturday morning. He was in this small restaurant and he was having, you know, an order of toast and coffee. And there were a number of people in the restaurant, an elderly couple, a man and a young wife and their child, but over on Dim's right there was a group of men sitting around a circular table and what Dim heard them talking about was, they were saying how difficult it is to train someone to fall over a dog. And later in the conversation, at some point all the men inexplicably said, "Amen, amen, amen." Dim heard that. But this amen has nothing to do with the story, it was just that Dim was there and remembered it all. And then later one of the men at the table mentioned corporate executives.

Well, as you know it takes two things to spark one idea and the statement about the tripping over dogs, along with the one about the corporate executives, came together as one magnificent business idea for Dim. He would train corporate executives how to trip over dogs and that was the beginning of his extraordinarily successful career because the great majority of corporate executives want to learn how to do this.

But it isn't easy to teach them. You can't just use a little dog because either the dog will bite your ankle, you know, or it will squeal piteously when you hit it with your foot. So Dim had to get some very serene Saint Bernards or perhaps some very old police dogs, ones that don't jump up anymore, setters or labrador retrievers, old retrievers. Well, anyway, Dim decided on large, amiable, aged dogs. And then he had to teach the executive, you know, how to trip without breaking the dog's ribs because you want to use the dog many times. Anyway, Dim figured this out and he offered workshops and retreats, convocations, everything, and—I'll explain it to you—the reason corporate executives want to learn how to trip over dogs is that, like everyone else, they want to be liked.

And what they wanted to do, for instance, was this. A corporate executive comes into a huge banquet hall filled with people all milling around and they all turn to see him and just as he gets to the door, he trips over a big dog. You can imagine the reaction of hundreds of women in that room when they see that, "Oh, he's a Du Pont, but he is as clumsy as my husband, the poor fellow." See, it elicits sympathy and every corporate executive wants sympathy and he wants people to like him. So Dim made a small fortune doing this, but it got so he had to hire, you know, accountants to go over the taxes and he had to have people setting up appointments, and so on, and one day he sat down and said, "Dim, is this the way you really want to spend your life?" And the small shining Dim inside of him said, "No, it isn't."

So Dim divested himself of his holdings, he gave his company over to a nephew of his. This nephew was a truck driver, so he was always called Semi Dim. And Semi was aggressive and made a very fine corporation out of all this effort, so that now he himself is a successful executive and has to trip over dogs. Dim, ah, let me see, Dim always had an interest, he received a small percentage of the profits because of the use of the Dim name. This is pretty much the story of his success in the business world.

The patent-leather slipper

You remember that Dim had that company where he
taught corporation executives how to trip over dogs? He
made a considerable fortune doing that. He had an interest
in the business even after he gave up the company to his
nephew, Semi Dim. Well, that made him a kind of a prize
or a catch. And Dim was not unhandsome, although he
was a bit on the plump side. But his weight was offset by
the fact that he had so much money. So, friends were
encouraging him to find someone and get married. And he
decided—he was not totally serious—he decided he would
have a great ball and perhaps would pick a wife from
among the women gathered there.

Anyway, that word was sent out and Dim rented the
Elks Club ballroom. This was before it was remodeled.
Well, that caused a flurry of excitment all over Sangamon
County. Every woman who could possibly get there got
there. They went with their brothers, fathers, mothers, their
indiscriminate dates, or whatever, even their boy friends, so
that they could be seen by Dim.

It was a pretty good dance. Dim had a 13-piece orches-
tra. As I remember, the Elks Club ballroom was a kind of
cavernous place, but not very elegant. Anyway, everyone

was dancing and Dim was socializing. Then suddenly into the hall came this beautiful girl, a girl in a bell-shaped golden dress. As she entered, there was a hush and then waves of astonishment swept over the hall as everybody fell back to observe her. There she was, this totally beautiful young girl, and Dim, because it was his ball, went boldly up to her and took her by the hand. The band struck up a majestic tune and they danced.

And everything was transformed. The cobwebbed shadows in the corners of the ceiling became peopled with small angel-like creatures in cream and ebony that gleamed with highlights of silver and gold. Where there had been gray walls, now there were banks of candles and great mirrors topped with smiling figurines. The room appeared twice, thrice, four, five times as large as it was. And this room was peopled by an ecstatic throng.

They were all fascinated by the girl in the bell-shaped gown. This girl was the daughter every mother had wanted and the sister every sister had wished for. She was the one they would have liked to have had instead of the one they got. And so they were all happy, and Dim was dancing with her, and he was totally enthralled.

Well, time went like the first creation. And then suddenly—it's very confusing at this point—the bells of the cathedral began to ring, bong bong bong. And, you see, there is a sort of an agreement that it must have been midnight. But some people say that it was 2:30, really, and some other people say that no, it was 10:40. And others argue that it was 11:27, which is mean star time. Nobody could agree. Some said, "No, no, no. Twelve o'clock is twelve o'clock." But they all agreed that whatever it was, it wasn't quite on the hour because the cathedral bells never rang on the hour, see, but there it was, bong bong bong.

The girl looked at her golden crystalline watch and said, "Oh, what's happening?"

And Dim said, "I think it's ringing midnight."

And now bong bong bong, nine strokes had sounded toward the hour. This girl put her hand over her mouth, which was opened in an expression of dismay, and before anybody could do anything, she turned and fled from the ballroom. Bong bong bong, there was the twelfth stroke!

The crowd was stunned. But Dim got his wits together and ran out after the girl. There was a doorman there, outside the Elks Club. Of course, the old Elks didn't have a doorman, but there was a man out there in connection with Dim's dance. And Dim asked, "Did you see the beautiful girl in a bell-shaped dress?"

This fellow scratched his chin, "No," he said. "I just saw a sort of mousy girl who was wearing blue jeans with the knees out and a soiled t-shirt. She got into a—the thing looked like an old Ford or a Toyota that had two hundred thousand miles on it." And he said, "You know, the funny thing was, I could swear there was a rat sitting right on top of the hood of that thing." And then he said, "Boy, that was a contrast. Because there was a girl came in here earlier looked like a young queen. She must have been a deb from somewhere, said her name was Ashley. She was riding in a reconstituted Duesenberg and her chauffeur wouldn't talk to you if you were human, you had to be some kind of a higher angelic spirit."

Dim was nonplussed. He didn't know what to make of this. He turned around to go back into the hall and there on the sidewalk was a patent-leather slipper. He picked it up, all that was left of that lovely girl he had danced with.

He was crushed, he thought maybe she'd give him a ring on the phone, or something. But after a number of days without a word from her at all, Dim thought, well, he'd put a notice in the paper that he would become perhaps espoused to whoever fit that slipper. See, he was smitten with love and he was not being very rational. So he had a kiosk put up on the south side of the Old State Capitol. And, you know, women came from all over Sangamon County and lined up on Sixth Street to try on the slipper.

I tell you, there were feet like no one had ever seen before. There were broad feet and narrow feet and stubby feet and long feet. There were feet with high arches and there were feet as flat as flapjacks. There were feet with bunions and feet with corns and feet with plantar's warts, some with ingrown toenails and some with long lacquered nails that looked like tiger claws. And do you know what those feet had in common? Every one of them fit the patent-leather slipper.

Can you imagine Dim's chagrin? What could he do? He was obliged to espouse the girl the patent-leather slipper fit. But it fit every woman in Sangamon County.

Well, they weren't humorous about it. Those women brought a class action suit against Dim because he had misled them. Yes, they sued him for breach of promise. And it stuck. Dim had to go to trial and, of course, the judge was amused and the jury felt the need to titter. The foreman couldn't resist saying that he who lasts last lasts best and the judge when he handed down the sentence noted that if the shoe fit, Dim would have to wear it. It wasn't their slipper. They could afford to smile.

Dim was conscientious. He paid off everyone that he could until finally he was broke and had to declare bankruptcy. So he lost that fortune, you see, but he still had the patent-leather slipper. He kept it on the mantel in the living room. Sometimes he would study it, wondering whatever happened to Ashley, whether she was one of those Sangamon County girls the slipper fit.

The tiny tarts

Well, you know one time Dim was in Covington, Kentucky, and he saw some graffiti on the walls there and they were sort of, oh, how would you describe them? Adolescent things. And they were all signed THE TINY TARTS. Dim thought, well those are probably fifth grade pom-pom girls or something, or then again maybe—Dim remembered the little dough cakes his mother used to make out of what was left over when she'd bake an apple pie, little things she'd put in muffin tins with dabs of strawberry or blueberry jam in them. She'd bake those and they were tiny tarts. Whatever. Dim figured this was a local thing and he wasn't worried about the tiny tarts at all. He returned to his home in central Illinois.

But shortly after that, now Dim is cautious here, he just says he was in a town north of where he lived and it was on a height. Well, that could be Mount Auburn or it could be Mount Pulaski or any of a number of towns up there—Blue Mound or Boody on the Shelbyville moraine. But what happened was, he came into this town and there weren't a lot of people out, except as he came down the street—he was just walking, looking at the churches, city hall, whatever you see in little Illinois towns, somebody's kindling wood. Well, you don't always have a lot of things to look at.

Anyway, Dim, all at once he was surrounded by these little girls. And they were all, you know, brushing against him and he—they had these pom-poms and batons—and he didn't know what was going on, whether he should be proud or humiliated. And then they started their little chant: "Tiny tarts tiny tarts, HA HA HA, tiny tarts tiny tarts TEE HEE HEE." Like that. And they began to throw their batons in the air and Dim didn't know whether to join in the fun or get out as fast as he could. But some of these batons were flaming at both ends and one came down and singed the hair over Dim's right ear, and then he knew it was time to cut out fast.

He began to run and all the little girls laughed with girlish derision. He ran for about a block before he turned around and noticed that nobody else was out. Well, a little boy came from one house and ran quickly across the street into another house—and then some parents came out to remonstrate with those girls, but Dim noticed that the parents kept looking over their shoulders for fear they would be hit with fiery batons. That's when Dim realized these girls were terrorizing the town.

He got out, sort of slunk out with his tail between his legs. But after he was back at his own place, he thought about what had happened to him and he became more and more furious to think that he should have been, you know, treated so shabbily by these fifth grade girls.

Then he began to rummage around in his old shed, his old garden shed, and do you know what he found there? He found one of those original sprinklers. Do you remember them? They were round brass rings, perforated, and you attached the hose and turned it on and the water sprang up in a huge crown on the lawn. It was a glorious thing to watch on a summer night, the crowns of water flowing out on the parched grass of the lawns.

Well, Dim got that and he made a harness so he could put it on his head, and then he got two five-gallon jugs, plastic jugs, and he attached hoses to them and he worked on a Y-joint so that the hoses entered into this brass crown, and then he got these hand pumps and he got this all together—it took him months to perfect because with any famous invention you have failures. But he finally got the thing so it would work and then he went back to that town.

I don't know whether it was Buffalo Hart or Clinton or Bulldog Crossing or Grove City, though about the only people in Grove City are in the cemetery, hardly enough to support a pom-pom society. Anyway, Dim went back there and strapped on his rig and walked down the lonesome main street of that town.

It wasn't long before the little girls were all out dancing around him, screaming and yelling,"Tiny tarts tiny tarts HA HA HA tiny tarts tiny tarts TEE HEE HEE." They had their batons lit, and Dim could see people were peeking out of their windows apprehensively. That's when he started to pump fiercely on the hand pumps, and the crown of water rose from his head and soaked those tiny tarts and put out their batons while they were still twirling in the air. They just came sizzling down to the ground and the pom-poms became like sodden mops you use in the basement. The tiny tarts' hair was hanging down in dripping clumps and those girls for all their ha ha's and tee hee's could only boo hoo. They were just boo hooing all around him.

Well, cheers sounded on the front porches and people came running from everywhere to congratulate Dim. And you know, they were quick to study his invention. They all built harnesses for themselves and went around with brass crowns on their heads, soaking those little girls until they almost drowned. So that was the end of the tiny tarts. As soon as they were outwitted like that, they all returned to being normal, lovely fifth grade girls and everything was just fine. It must have been like a Salem Village syndrome. They could have had bad wheat or something.

The townspeople were so appreciative that they built a park named for Dim. It was called Dim Park. And it was a place full of shady trees and little apparatuses for children to climb on, and wives liked to stay there with their little ones, and old men would sit and read the Sunday paper there, and even teenagers would come down and throw frisbees. But it's a funny thing, to this day no fifth grade girl has a ever entered that park. Isn't that strange? That's the truth.

The python hound

Did you know that Dim had a dog before he had old
Sleuth? Yes, he went down to Belleville one time and he
met a fellow there who ran a kennel. This fellow sold Dim
a pedigreed python hound. Yes. Dim brought it back up
with him, it didn't look extraordinary. This fellow explained
about these python hounds to Dim, they're German dogs.
You know in Belleville there are still people who come up
to you and say, "Hey, you vant a dozen eggs dis morgan?"
So it was natural this man would have a German dog and
the dog's name was Kurt Hunt. Dim used to call him, you
know, "good fellow" and "old boy," he very seldom referred to him as "Kurt Hunt."

Well, anyway, the kennel owner said these dogs, there
are very few of them in the world, are a very special breed.
They are just bred to fight pythons. And, you see, one of
the ways they do this is—when attacked by a python they
can excrete little oily substances in their fur, so as the
snake tries to coil around one or another of them, it slips
off. This has a side effect. If a python hound gets a flea
bite, the oil appears locally where the flea is and when the
dog rolls over, the flea drowns. So they're not bothered by

fleas very much. Also, these python hounds have retractable tails because the python likes to sneak up and bite them, grab ahold of their tails, see, and then swallow them, and by a genetic adjustment over the years this particular breed can retract the tail.

Dim made the mistake of coming back to his home town and going to the pharmacy and telling everybody about this python hound with these characteristics. Well, everybody just guffawed. They thought it was ridiculous, especially considering the dog that Dim brought with him. It was a nondescript dog, it had a sort of mousy, kind of a mange-like, coat, you know, and its ears looked like, well, you've seen those long john doughnuts. And its tail was askew, it was always sort of at 20 after 4 instead of 6:30. In fact people would say, "If you could stand him on end, Dim, you could use him to open up bottles of wine." They made comments like that. And the dog's belly hung down. They'd say, "That dog needs to be jacked up in the middle. Why don't you go to the vet and have a splint put on him?" They would make those kinds of criticisms and that would have been all right if it was a short-legged dog, like a dachshund. But this dog had long legs and looked like it was swaybacked.

Well, of course, there were no pythons around, so how could Dim prove this was a genuine python hound? And with no pythons around, the dog got into a bad habit, it would attack the neighbors' hoses, tear up the garden hoses. And after awhile people started taking their old garden hoses and throwing them over into Dim's yard, until it looked like a Knights of Columbus hall after a spaghetti dinner. Yes. So Dim had to keep the dog in the house, but to content it he went down to a toy store and bought a snake, a huge snake about 20 feet long. It was one of those fuzzy stuffed snakes and the dog had a wonderful time just horsing around with it. He'd pull the head off every once in a while and Dim would have to take it up to the square where there were some ladies who made drapes and things like that and they would sew the head back on for him. So that's the way it was, everybody was amused, you know, and as long as he didn't tear up their garden hoses, people could tolerate Dim's nondescript dog.

And life would have gone on like that and Dim would have been humiliated and embarrassed because he had been taken in by that kennel owner in Belleville. But! The time came one summer night when a Venezuelan circus drove into town and they pitched their tents up on the ball diamond near the old mine pond. And everybody—well, Dim didn't go, he was a little under the weather, but everybody else was there, watching the trapeze acts and the jugglers and the elephants, and suddenly those Venezuelans began to yell, "Madre mia! Caramba! Serpiente boa!"

Some thoughtless attendant had left the latch open on the python's cage and it had gotten out and immediately it went after the mayor. People had mixed reactions about that. Those who had voted for the mayor were appalled while those who had voted against him were, you know, willing to see how the contest came out. They had an objective attitude. Well, anyway, the mayor, he got away finally and the snake slithered from the tent out into the dark of the night. Everyone was frightened because this snake was loose and it would eat up their pets and maybe go after some of the children. And nobody knew where the thing was.

There was a hue and cry and lots of wringing of hands and then somebody said, "Why don't we go down and get Dim's python hound? Maybe that dog can do something." So they all nodded their heads and went and knocked on Dim's door and told him about the loose python.

Dim said, "Well, all right, I'll bring him up."

But, you know, the dog didn't want to go out. He was watching some other dogs on television. Dim had to put a leash on him and they had to drag the animal because it was cool inside and the show was pretty good. They had to force him into the car. And when they brought him up and he got out, he was whimpering around, you know, looking just like he always did.

Then suddenly he caught the scent of the python and that dog changed right before their eyes. He became aggressive, his ears went up and his scrawny old tail. He trembled with excitement, sniffed here and sniffed there and finally he came to a point in front of a culvert under the railroad tracks and he went in there. I should tell you about this dog. The way he used to bark, he would go "Whoo ooo oo. Whoo ooo oo" like he was always running down, you know. But when he went into that culvert, there were all kinds of fierce barks, howls, growls, yaks, everything you ever heard of, and everybody stood there waiting—it was like the mongoose going into the hole for a cobra, very dangerous.

Then all at once with a terrifying hiss the python burst out of the culvert and grabbed its own tail and rolled in a hoop as fast as it could back into the tent and into its own cage and pulled the door shut behind itself. And a moment later out pranced Dim's python hound with his pricked up ears and his belly up and his back straight and he had this glistening black coat shining with tufts of gold and his tail was like a deer's scut straight up behind him and he leaped about, marking a bush here and a rock there. He marked everything and everybody applauded because they knew no python was going to slither where that dog had been.

Well, Dim felt a lot different about Kurt after that, he didn't feel bad for himself and his dog anymore. And ever after that, people were pretty circumspect when they talked about Dim and his python hound.

The little green man

Dim bought an old house. At one time it was a nicely kept place, he was happy with it. But, you know, those old houses have the strangest heating systems, so if you're in the upstairs front bedroom, you can hear what everybody is chatting about when they are frying some eggs in the kitchen, this kind of thing. Well, after Dim had lived in the house a month, oh, was it a month? A month and a half, I guess. He was up taking a bath and it was a funny business, what he heard. He was taking a bath and he heard, it sounded like a toy harmonica, someone was playing "Come Back To Erin, Mavourneen." That's what he heard. It was the most sorrowful sound, Dim almost cried in the tub. But he was almost through with his bath anyway, so he got out and patted himself off. He thought the sound must have come from a closet, but he didn't find anything in the closets except some old shoes.

    You know, that kept up. It wasn't a loud noise, it was the sort of thing that registers in the back of your mind and whenever you're not thinking of something else, you hear it—"Come with the shamrocks and springtime, Mavourneen." Dim was bothered by it, as you can guess. But he didn't want the word to get out that he was hearing a ghost or something in his house. So he went to the town square, went to a cafe that had round tables and a magazine rack. You could buy a copy of *The Rolling Stones* there and people used to drink lots of coffee and chat. Well anyway, Dim went there. He didn't want to be obvious, but he really wanted to know if there had been reports about his house, that people heard "Come Back to Erin, Mavourneen" in his house, played on the harmonica. But it's hard to disguise what you want to know if that's what it is. Folks managed to guess what Dim wanted and they'd say things like, "Well, no, I never heard of anybody in that house playing a creepy harmonica, but you know, over on the east side of town there's a guy in a two-story brick house that plays Bach fugues on the double bass. Yeah, he's been doing that since the Civil War. But he's terrible, nobody pays any attention to him. Old Fiddle Fingers, that's what they call him. Plays whenever there's an eclipse." They'd roll their eyes and say things like that.

But where was I? Oh, yes. Dim had to endure this kind of talk. But one day he was down in his basement, he was pouring water into his furnace, it was an old coal burner converted to gas with a water collar in it to help with humidity. Well, Dim was down there doing that, he had a garden hose wired up to the water collar so all he had to do was twist the nozzle, and he heard just as plain as a winter day "Come Back to Erin" on the harmonica. The sound was coming from behind the furnace.

Dim got a trouble light and poked around back there, it was just a limestone crawl space wall back there, but he heard the sound of the harmonica coming from those stones. He got out his pocket knife and he worked the mortar around the stones. Sure enough, one stone was quite loose and he managed to pull it out. Then he took his trouble light and held it in front of the hole and do you know what he saw? This little green man in there with a harmonica. He was just holding the harmonica in front of his mouth, and his knees were drawn up against his chest because he was so cramped in this little chamber and he was staring out into the light and there was terror in his eyes. Dim realized that anyone so afraid might have a heart attack or something, whatever would happen to a little green man. I don't suppose you would want to know what Dim said? He thought quickly and said to the little green man, "Would you like to have a cup of tea?"

At this, the little green man smiled. "Ah!" he said, "You pronounced the magic words." And always afterward the little green man started his sentences with that "ah!" as if he had eaten a mess of peas and shamrocks and they didn't sit too well on his little stomach. But, anyway, Dim reached in and took him out, he was just a little thing, and carried him upstairs and put him on the kitchen table. Then he got two boxes of hot roll mix and placed them on the table and this gave the little green man a a little bench to sit on with some dignity. He was quite small. Well, Dim gave him a cup of tea, he had a thimble that he used, which was all right except that it was metal and a little hot. Dim didn't have a porcelain thimble, just a plain thimble because once in a while he'd lose a button on his shirt or something like that and have to sew it back on. Of course, if he was sewing a patch on a pair of corduroy pants, he'd need a thimble because the needle eye might stick in his hand, it would be hard to push through the material if he was sewing a pocket or a cuff, don't you see?

What were we saying? I don't remember how this story goes. Oh, yes, the little green man was drinking tea. Well, Dim told him that he had been up to the town square and nobody remembered anyone playing a harmonica in this house and the little green man said, "Ah! I was just beginning to play the harmonica." You have to understand that the little green man had been sealed up in that hole since the time the house was built, and the house was well over a hundred years old, it went way back to a Van Buren land grant in the 1830s. But the little green man wasn't able to play the harmonica until he was released from an old curse.

Now it all began—now this is the little green man talking to Dim and, you remember, Dim had it written down in one of his spiral notebooks—he used to number his stories. I think this one was number 43 or 44, something like that, and he had a little tablet with the numbers opposite the titles of the stories, also. He wrote with a pen, usually, in blue ink, though sometimes he would forget and use red ink.

As it turned out, in the old days this little green man was a member of a little green man immigrant train. They were going west and they got as far as a spot of high ground just on the left side of the road and several miles this side of Taylorville and before you get to Kincaid. You have to understand, though, at that time Taylorville was a couple of cabins and Kincaid was a place where deer slept up above the Sangamon River. Some people say it's not much more today, but I don't know anything about that.

Well, they were coming through there and it was the little green man's wedding night. Now these little green men are not Christians, but they have sort of Christian-like rituals. He would have been married, but the little green man, Dim's friend, I mean, committed the unpardonable sin. He reached into his weskit, little green men all used to wear weskits, into the pocket and could not produce the ring. He knew he had it when he came to the place where they had circled the wagons for the wedding. I should say there were also little green women present, of course, because he was going to marry one. He loved her, her name was Brigid. Dim's little green man had a name, too, and Dim would have remembered it, but it was all full of vowels and consonants. He never could keep them straight, said you had to have a flannel mouth to be able to pronounce that name.

But about the ring, the little green man knew he had it, but he didn't have it when he reached for it. Well, Brigid's father rose into a towering rage and he said, "You will never have the hand of my daughter Brigid in matrimony until you can produce that ring." And so, a week or so later when the ring still wasn't found, they put him in the hole in the basement where Dim discovered him.

Now you may understand that Brigid's father O'Toone, Joseph O'Toone, probably didn't care whether the little green man found the ring or not, probably never approved of the wedding in the first place, but I don't know that he realized how vindictive he was. It would take a lot of psychoanalysis to determine a thing like that. Of course, Dim didn't write everything down and for all I know, Joseph O'Toone picked his prospective son-in-law's pocket.

Well, what happened was the ring really was lost and rains came and covered up the spot where it was. Years later there was a dump where the little immigrant train had circled on that sad night, but then came a temporal coincidence. About a month and a half after Dim moved into his old house, there were heavy rains over by Kincaid and the ridge where the ring was got a good drubbing and the ring was exposed right where the little green man had lost it more than a hundred years before. Then Brigid, because of a loophole in the anti-feminist rules of the green man clan that made a daughter almost the total property of her father, then Brigid, once it was possible to find the ring, could appear in a vision to tell her beloved where it was. And by the same dispensation her beloved man, the little green man, was allowed to play the harmonica whenever he pleased, which if you remember is how Dim came to find him. All things are possible in this world, as Dim used to say.

What was there to do? Dim went over to the Kincaid dump and went right through the dump and up on the ridge and located the ring without any trouble at all because the morning sun was gleaming on it. It was really some kind of marvel because that ring was no bigger than a contact lens. Two pro football teams crawling around on a football field wouldn't have been able to find a contact lens that small if, say, a defensive end had lost it during a play-off.

Well, Dim brought the ring back and the little green man, he was extravagant with glee, jumping up and down, playing "Cucka Nandio" on his harmonica.

At this point Dim became facetious, really, and he said, "Now I know that you little green men have this pot of gold."

The little green man took such a deep breath he almost swallowed his harmonica. "Ah, no, no!" he said.

But Dim, see the difference between Dim and other people is that Dim was not hoggish about money. He would never have caught a little green man by the leg and held onto him until the whereabouts of a crock of gold was revealed. And, you know, that little green man sat there on top of the two boxes of hot roll mix and thought a while and then he drew his knees up and wrapped his arms around them and he looked at Dim and he said, "You will have your golden surprise because Padraic O'Haughenomaughnees never will forget a favor." And you know, just like that he disappeared, just in the flip of a fly wing on your fingertip.

Well, Dim put the boxes of hot roll mix away, somewhat regretfully. He didn't—this is a very long story, anyone reading it, his patience would run out, I think, but I am putting it down pretty much the way Dim had it. Let's see, yes, Dim didn't give much thought to the little green man's promise. How could you take a person who sat on two boxes of hot roll mix seriously?

But, you know, it was about a month after and Dim was drowsing in the morning with the sunlight just slipping into the bedroom window and do you know what he heard? Why it was a harmonica playing "At the Risin' of the Moon" and he knew that the little green man was somewhere about. Well, he put on his slippers and bathrobe and came down and opened the side door, but there was no one to be seen, there was no little green man, there was nothing.

Then he looked at the picnic table on the porch and there was this lamp. It was a lamp like something out of the Arabian Nights, an exotic thing, and you will say, "How did a lamp get in this story of the little green man, Padraic O'Haughenomaughnees?" Well, I don't know. All I know is it was there and Dim wondered at it. It was a little dusty, so Dim brought it into the kitchen and got a nice soft cloth and was rubbing the dust off of it when suddenly out of the spout came this huge genie. He was so big he had to bend over half way across the kitchen ceiling. He tried to support himself, you know, by leaning against the kitchen table, but the legs snapped under his weight. Do you know what he said? You will never guess what a genie would say if he broke a kitchen table. He said, "Oops!"

Well, Dim invited him into the dining room, which had a much higher ceiling, so he was more comfortable and the genie looked at Dim and he said, "You will have three wishes."

Dim was flabbergasted, he didn't know what was best to say, so he said, "Oh, a million dollars."

The genie said, "You have it." Then the genie said, "And what is your second wish?"

And Dim had lost all powers of imagination. All he could do was, "Oh, ah, oh, how about another million?"

And the genie said, "You have it. And your third wish?"

And Dim said, "Oh, another million."

And the genie said, "It is yours." And with that he disappeared.

So you see that Dim's friend Padraic O'Haughenomaughnees did keep his word. You probably want to know, I mean the story could end here and we would enjoy—something in us would respond to the fact that the little green man had not forgotten his promise. But I suppose you will want to know what Dim did with the money. He, ah, he thought he'd like to count it and he figured how he would do that. If he counted a hundred bills at a time, now this is allowing for him occasionally to turn one over and look at the back of it, it would take him perhaps two minutes to count a hundred bills. One's, I mean, one-dollar bills, three million one's.

He divided, he wanted to see, you know, so he divided what? A hundred into three million. And he got 30,000 from that, so that would represent 30,000 hundred-dollar packets full of one's. Then he figured it took two minutes to count each packet, so if there were 30,000, it would take 60,000 minutes, right? Well, he only wanted to spend two hours a night, so he needed to make all this into units of two, so he divided and what did he get? Well, wait, he divided 120 minutes, you see, for the two hours, into the 60,000 and he got 500. So he had to spend 250 evenings at two hours an evening to count the three million dollars, which he did. Of course, he didn't count on Sundays and he never counted during commercials, so you can imagine how long it took.

But you know, he had friends who came over and helped him. Good neighbors, see, small towns have good neighbors, they come over when they think you need some help. They would wrap the hundred-dollar packets up with paper bindings and then scotch tape each binding and Dim had a friend in a company that had a duplicating department and the friend would bring the empty boxes from there. Dim always liked to put the money in the same kinds of boxes, he was neat about such things.

I suppose you want to know what Dim did during the commercials? You know what he did? Why he would get out his harmonica and sit there and play "We're in the Money." Wasn't that disgusting? But he always ended with a reel in honor of Padraic and Brigid O'Toone-O'Haughenomaughnees. The little green people always doubled surnames when they married. They had the better of us there, don't you think? But I guess I should stop here, Dim didn't have anything else to say about all this.

Wind and the tomcats

Well, then there is the famous story of the rough night of south wind. That's when the wind really blew up in recurring gale-like swaths through the town. It woke Dim at about two o'clock in the morning, so he got up and looked out the window above the street. He stared out, watching for tornadic clouds. Suddenly he saw the wind blow with such force that it flattened all the trees north and then it let up to gather strength and come on again, but at that point all the trees swung back south and they hit that wind, just as it was ready for another onslaught, and they drove it back in a kind of reverse spiral on itself. And there it was, whirling around and around level to the street, just about six or seven inches off the pavement for a block and a half. It was eerie looking.

Then Dim saw the strangest thing. It seemed that there was a pair of tomcats at the west end of that spiraling wind and they were in a terrible raging tomcat fight, and at the same time there was another pair of tomcats and they were at the eastern end of this wind and they were in a terrible fight. Then suddenly both pairs of cats were sucked into the very center of that wind and they smacked together all at once at the same time and there was a terrifying, horrible noise and claws, chunks of thunder, fur, lightning, every-thing, shot out of the center of the storm like a gas bag exploding.

Well, whenever Dim told that story, he liked to add a little moral, he would always say at the end, "So if you are a tomcat and want to fight another tomcat, you should be sure there aren't two other tomcats fighting at the same time at the other end of a horizontal tornado because you might get yourself blown to pieces in the wind." Everybody would feel righteous, just thinking about it.

Dim and the phone call

I think that the first time I heard about Dim was in connection with a long distance phone call he got from Washington, D.C., just about when he was ready to sit down to dinner. There was a person on the phone who was into some hard salesmanship to sell him a book on gardening. Dim was a little peeved and he said, "Well, look, we don't need any books on gardening out here. The soil is so fertile that our problem is to cut things back. If you can get us a book on how to contain the growth of our gardens, that would be a bestseller out here."

Well, that didn't deter her and so Dim said, "Look, only the other day a red raspberry bush reached out and grabbed two of the children and their folks had to call the rescue squad to beat the bush back for about two hours before it would release the kids."

Well, this lady was a little peeved herself when she heard Dim tell about the raspberry bush, but she kept on, told him that if he bought this book he'd have miracles of tomatoes, and all that.

And Dim said, "Look, we still have a basement full of beans from two years ago, we just can't eat enough of them." And then he went on, he said there was a lady down in Virden took some of those fertility pills and she had, she had six little ones. And it would have been, you know, very uncomfortable for them except that the first day her husband was able to make a cradle out of a huge pumpkin that he got out of the garden. And then Dim told her, "We have to watch out, you know, that the policemen don't fall asleep on the beets here."

She was furious when she heard that and she said, "I don't have time to sit here and waste my phone call just to hear you making these dumb stories up."

"Well," Dim said, "I didn't call you. I'm just telling you the truth, this is the way it is here. You have to broadcast the corn high here because it's already beginning to root before it gets into the ground."

She hung up then, so that kind of ended this story. But Dim thought about it, he figured that if you maybe shot corn out of shotgun barrels so it went high enough into the air, it would already have silk on the ears by the time it got to the ground and then if you could just catch it, you wouldn't even have to plant it. But he was never able to make that a reality as far as I know.

Sleuth and the rabbit

Well, you may know that Dim had a wonderful dog by the name of Sleuth. This dog was about 17 or 18 years old. Dim found him in a national park one time and brought him home. The dog lived a mild enough life around the house, but on this one occasion he spotted a big rabbit in the yard and he took out after that rabbit and the rabbit went east toward the rising sun. Dim chased Sleuth for a while, an old dog like that you don't want getting lost on the other side of town. But old Sleuth went "gahoo gahoo gahoo gahoo" as a dog will. Sounded like a—kind of like a church bell warming up for a wedding. And he disappeared on the trail of this rabbit.

And that was the last Dim saw of him for four years and then one evening about 7:30 as the sun was setting, Dim heard Sleuth coming out of the west. It sounded like—Dim sort of remembered the church bell gahooing—and sure enough there was Sleuth wagging his tail up on the step outside the kitchen door. But he wasn't really gahooing, he was going "wong wong wong wong wong wong wong wong." That's the way Chinese dogs bark, so Dim figured that Sleuth had chased the rabbit around the world and they had spent some time in China.

Dim went out in the yard then and there was that rabbit. Now you think, how did he know it was the same rabbit? It's because that particular rabbit had a broken right front leg, which had healed up badly, and it kind of stuck out. This rabbit was no good on short hops, he'd sort of keel over to the right. But on the long hops he could leap five, six feet. He was really a great jumping rabbit.

Dim told some of his friends that he knew it anyway, that this was the rabbit that had been to China because it had this little straw hat on. "They wear them when they plant rice in the paddies over there," he said.

His neighbors couldn't argue with that. So that's the story of Sleuth and the rabbit.

The night Sugar Creek got lost

Now this is—some of you may know we've had terrible
rain of late and that reminds me of the time Dim was over
there on Route 104 coming home from a party and he saw
that Sugar Creek had wandered out of its banks and
couldn't find its way back in. So he rushed into town and
told everybody they had better get out and start looking for
Sugar Creek. Well, nobody in Auburn would buy a story
like that, so he went down to Thayer and everybody came
out. They had all kinds of kerosene lanterns and electric
lights, you know, and what not, and they hoo-ha'd and
halloo'd all over the territory out there looking for Sugar
Creek. Never did find it. But there was a report that it was
seen somewhat east of Divernon and it was making the
most sorrowful gurgling sound because it seemed to know
that it was getting near to Pawnee and might find a bed
there and the last place it wanted to bed down was in
Pawnee.

Easter dinner and the ducks

This is another one of those rain stories where you have so much rain, it causes strange things to happen. On this occasion Dim was having an Easter dinner. He had guests over, there must have been maybe 12 or 13 people and he got out an extra table and set it all up. He had daffodils, two bowls of daffodils down the length of the board. It was very pretty and attractive and Dim made a big bean pot, a bean pot for the occasion. It was like a Boston baked bean pot, except that where in the Boston pot they put in molasses, Dim always used maple syrup. Oh, you've got the onion in there and the bacon and the maple syrup and the beans and all, and what else? Sugar and mustard, things like that. It was really delicious. So he set that out and he made some kashadi. I should say here that he always used Funks Grove sirrup, even spelled the way they do in Funks Grove, because he had local loyalty. But anyway he made some kashadi, which is just a plain little dish of brown rice and black-eyed peas with a little salt that they use in India as a kind of breakfast dish, but it goes very well with the bean pot.

Well, everybody was having a good time at this dinner except there was so much rain that right in the middle of it, a bunch of ducks swam in through the windows of the dining room and kept swimming back and forth right at the chin level of the guests. And then one of the ducks waggled its tail and got water in Dim's eyes and Dim told the other guests that he thought that one was the unkindest duck of all. See, he was, he had read his *Julius Caesar* and he was quoting Shakespeare. The other adults were embarrassed, but they were glad that the children didn't have to hear Dim. You see, the children were eating down below the water level, so they couldn't hear the conversation. Dim said later that they were the best behaved children. Only one of them complained that the corn bread was a little soggy that day.

I Ching and Brandy

One day I Ching felt a little sporty for a rabbit and he decided he'd like to hop somewhere. And, you know, I Ching's hop was really a limp because, remember, he had that broken right foreleg that was healed up. Anyway, he hopped sportfully along a little out of his territory, up north a block and a couple of blocks east, and he came to this yard that was a kind of rabbit's delight. It had foliage everywhere and plants all over the place and it had a big fence around it, but a rabbit that had circumnavigated the world, of course, would have no trouble with a tall picket fence. So, I Ching went on into the yard.

Well, there were a number of dogs that lived in that yard, but fortunately for I Ching some delivery man had left the gate open that morning and all but one had gotten loose and they were every which way over the township. The owners had gone out after them because these dogs all had papers. They were very remarkable dogs. As a matter of fact they were pedigreed basset hounds. Well, you know how a basset hound doesn't run, it lumbers—it is sort of like a freight going by in the evening on an old track and you can see these freight cars groaning from side to side and down and up—well, that's the way basset hounds run.

And, of course, one of their distinguishing features is they have these incredibly long ears that hang down and almost touch the ground on either side.

So anyway, I Ching came in and those dogs were all out, as I said, they were scattered everywhere. But there was one dog left, a young female by the name of Brandywine. Everybody called her Brandy and when I Ching came in, she saw him. Brandy had bad eyesight, she couldn't see very well and she thought, "What a wonderful companion." And I Ching was big for a rabbit. I won't say that she thought, "What a wonderful dog," mistaking I Ching for a dog, but there was just something in her that responded to this big benevolent shape coming towards her.

Well, you know, they had a real frolic together for about an hour and a half in that yard and then I Ching left. He thought, "Oh, it was a great scene but you know —" I Ching was something of a fatalist, he didn't believe in repeating a good thing. And it was lucky for him he didn't go back when the rest of the dogs were there. I'm not saying a rabbit would think something like this, but that's what Dim wrote down, perhaps for the sake of the story.

Well, it's unusual for a rabbit and a dog to sport about together, so a number of people passing by had stopped to watch and they told the owners, the couple who owned Brandy. And about two or three weeks later, well, it was obvious that Brandy was pregnant and these owners were furious. They went down and complained to Dim that his rabbit had come over and impregnated their dog.

And Dim told them, "Look, it's a wild rabbit, it isn't as if he slept here in the kitchen at night and he certainly never comes to the door for handouts. It just happens that he and I live on the same property."

Well, these people, they realized they couldn't hold Dim liable for something that a wild rabbit that lived in his yard had done on their property. Who would be safe? Anyway, the time came and Brandy delivered and the pups looked just like basset hounds except that their ears stood straight up. It was ridiculous. The owners were furious again. They could have killed Dim and every rabbit in the town. But, you know, the word got around and pretty soon they were getting telegrams and letters from everywhere in the world. The Orient was interested in this I Ching that had impregnated a dog and they got an offer from the zoo in Vienna. The zoo there sent this telegram in which they referred to the Hare Basset Hounds. Other people called them "rasset hounds" and things like that.

But the offers were hard and fast because this was a genetic marvel I Ching and Brandy had wrought. The owners sold the puppies all around the world and got a very good price, too, no question about that, so they felt a lot better about what had happened. And people around town say there hasn't been anything like that since the jack rabbits came out of Oklahoma into the Ozarks one hot summer in 1857 and created the Missouri mule. So that's the story of I Ching and Brandy.

The kitten in the soft maple

One evening in late May, it was just before sunset, Dim was out cutting some flowers in his front yard. He had some nice deep blue irises that he liked to cut each year. Put some on the kitchen table. Anyway, he was out there when he heard this pitiful meowing. It sounded like a kitten wanting to adopt someone. Dim looked around but he didn't see anything. Finally he figured out that the kitten was trapped high up in the soft maple. Now these soft maples put out many branches. They don't fork too well, but each one makes almost a forest of its own. Dim's tree must have been 60 or 70 feet high and the kitten was up there a good 25 feet.

So Dim went over to one of his neighbors who had a cherry picker. You have to know what a cherry picker is. If you see telephone linemen working on the high wires, they're in a kind of a—it looks like a big trash bucket on the end of a hydraulic lift. So they're up there with all their wirecutters and they're protected in this big bucket. They call that a cherry picker because you could use one to get up and pick the high cherries in the fruit trees, you see. But the cherry picker Dim's neighbor had wasn't quite like that. It was the kind they use to wash windows up on three and four and five story buildings. It's a hydraulic lift, but it has one of those wire mesh cages instead of a bucket. Well, Dim got his friend to bring his truck down from Springfield. He hoisted Dim right up about 25 feet and there Dim was in this cage, looking at the little kitten. He said the usual things like, "Here kitty, kitty, here kitty," but the cat wouldn't come. The little thing was so pitiful. Its bones were sticking out, you know, its ribs were sticking out through the fur and it had these big, glazed eyes in its head staring at Dim and it still went, "meow meow." Dim figured that the cat was afraid of him, but it was also very hungry. So he had his friend ease him back to the ground and he went and got a saucer of milk and his friend put him right up again next to the little kitten. This time the kitten took one look at the saucer and leaped right at it, its heart just purring in gratitude as it lapped up the milk.

Well, this would have been the end of the story, but by now the sun had gone down and it was dark. And reflected in the light of the street lamp Dim saw 39 pairs of eyes. Other cats in the tree had all come down to watch the kitten, watch rather greedily this kitten lapping the milk. Now Dim really didn't know whether it was 39 ordinary cats or 78 one-eyed cats he was looking at—he couldn't see so well in the darkness. Or again, whether it was some kind of combination where you might have, you know, 20 two-eyed cats and then the remainder would be one-eyed. The mathematics of it, Dim used to say, got just too complicated to figure out so he was never quite sure, because of that, how many cats were up in the tree. But when he saw all those cats, he came back down again and he told his friend that they would have to make some kind of arrangement to get a lot more milk because the whole tree was full of cats.

Well, various people had gathered as they do in a small town whenever something unusual happens. They talked this over among themselves and the consensus was that those cats had achieved some kind of a Golden Age in the soft maple. People frequently talk about that kind of thing—the Golden Age—in small towns. Everybody knew that those cats would never come back down into the harsh world of dogs and boys tossing them in the air to see how they would land in puddles and things like that. So Dim had himself hoisted up on the lift again and he rigged a pulley and a rope and he got one of those—it wasn't a bucket, it was more like an old style—I remember them as aluminum. They were dish washers before people had those special dish washing machines. Just a big, shallow-bottomed aluminum vessel you washed your dishes in. Dim clamped four pliers on it and taped them tight and shut. Then he knotted lines to the pliers so that the dishpan—that's what it used to be called, a dishpan—would be kept level.

And every other evening they filled it with milk and hoisted it up to the cats. Of course the aggressive ones, the 39 or 78 or how many there were—54, maybe—they'd jump right onto the rim of that big pan and lap up the milk. There was just a chorus of wonderful purring, you could hear it from blocks away. But the others, the older cats maybe or the ones with arthritis, they'd wait until those were done and then they'd just flop right into the milk. We know this because of Dim's notes. He liked to study them off the porch with binoculars. They'd flop in and then they'd get out and lick themselves off. That's how they got their milk.

It really was wonderful, Dim used to say, because those cats weren't the only creatures in that tree. Those soft maples are ecological gardens of Eden. Dim's was full of fox squirrels, for instance, and there were several snakes in the bole and certainly pigeons and starlings and field sparrows and creepers and flycatchers and flickers and always a robin or two, bluejays, catbirds, as well as carpenter ants and hundreds of bugs. They all got along just fine. Dim, he used to think about that, saying if we only knew how to imitate the harmony of those creatures in the soft maple, we'd all be better off.

Now, some questions have come up, there are some questions. How the lines were gathered, for instance, from the four pliers. Dim secured them in a Turk's head about three feet above the dishpan. It's true that in the beginning the pan just swung in the air beneath the pulley and some of the less agile cats fell off the rim. But Dim and several friends hammered a platform about four feet under the pulley and Dim reset the pulley on a swivel arm, which wasn't easy, so they would only have to haul the milk up and then swing the pan down on the platform. After that no more cats fell out of the tree. It is also true that in the beginning Dim hauled the milk up by himself. But really it took a couple of people. It was heavy—the milk was, you know. And for a while some newspaper boys did it. But later to insure continuity and steadfastness the members of the Sertoma Club took over the chore.

So that's how the cats were fed in the soft maple. Oh yes, I should add that they always fed the cats in the evening, according to Dim, because in the mornings most people are out walking around. Some people walk in the evenings, but in the evenings most people like to ride their bicycles. It sounds strange, but the people who didn't own bicycles, they were the ones who used to go over to Dim's and haul up the milk for the cats. As for the milk, some local cows were used to provide it and there was no problem at all because if one cow ran out of milk, they'd just bring another one over.

Catfish gardening

One time Dim got a strange ear itch, so he went up to Springfield to a dermatologist and the dermatologist examined him and prescribed some salve and said, "You put that on every day for about a month and the itch will disappear." So Dim wanted to know if he could put this salve on and still swim in Lake Springfield. The dermatologist said he didn't see why not and at this point, Dim told him how he took the silt home from the lake to use in his French-intensive shower. The doctor was fascinated by that and he said, "Listen, have you ever tried taking those 20-pound catfish in Lake Springfield and using them when you plant? Just put one in at the bottom of the seed bed."

Well, Dim thought this over and figured it was probably a pretty good idea, so he went out at night in a boat. He went out at night because, he said, he didn't want the catfish to see the lines, just the doughballs, and he caught a mess of these catfish and he went back—it was in April— and he put them in the cornrows, sort of like the way the Narragansetts taught the pilgrims to do, only they used small fish, not big 20-pound catfish.

The result of all this is that he grew these immense rows of corn. In fact, when the silk came out of the ears, you know, it was like comets, just pointing down toward the earth. You won't believe this, but some of those ears weighed a hundred pounds and he had to ask some teenagers to help him harvest. And then there was no way to get the cornstalks down except with a power saw. He had to pay to have that done, but there he made a little profit because he was able to sell it for 40 bucks a cord, so he was pretty happy about that. But he said he was glad he cut the fish in half. He said, "What would have happened if I had a whole catfish for every kernel of seed corn?" He said, "We'd of had a forest of redwoods out here and I never would have been able to find my way through the yard." So that's that story.

Dim in Camelot

This is a strange story. It requires great sympathy on the part of readers. You may remember that there was a time when Dim was standing on the shore of Lake Springfield at sundown and the light was glittering on the little waves because there was a little wind up and that glitter was in his eyes and he saw out in the middle of the lake he didn't know what. A duck flopping down or was it a gull diving for a fish? But it seemed that at the moment this object came down, something emerged from the lake, too, and took hold of it and Dim thought, "Why it's an arm catching ahold of a great sword and taking it back down into the water!"

Well, he discounted, you know, what he had just seen. Reminded him of something he had read when he was a schoolboy, a medieval thing like that. But as he was sitting on the broken concrete that lines the shore of the lake, he looked down and noticed this bottle. It was sealed and corked, but he saw that it had a message in it and he took his pen knife and dug at the cork and poked in there and pulled out a little piece of parchment. There was writing on it. It said, "You will appear at Willemore when the Cherry is there." And Dim thought, "This is very curious."

And then, of course, he forgot all about Lake Spring-field at sundown and the bottle until one afternoon he was driving west on Cherry Road and he came to this place where it said Willemore and he was amazed. You know, Cherry Road goes over from Chatham to MacArthur. So he stopped his car and got out and there, right there close to that intersection was an old Chevrolet with five people in it and they were all dressed in armor.

That startled Dim and he said, "Well, what are you fellows up to?" What else would you say?

And, you know, the driver told him. He said, "We belong to the Society for Creative Anachronism and we're off to a joust in Rochester." Dim could see they were dressed like knights. But there was this old man in the back seat staring at him. He had a golden beard and his eyes were like points of blue ice.

He put a claw on Dim's arm and said, "Find M.P. Tell him it is all right."

Then the driver said, "Yes, the four of us are going to Rochester and we're going to beat the farcing out of those people over there in the joust." And he drove off.

But Dim said to himself, "There were five in that car."

Well, what do you think of a thing like that? Dim knew there was certainly a discrepancy and for several days after he wondered about the old man and his message. How was he going to go about finding M.P.? He didn't know what to do. But it turned out when he was in the library—he liked when he was in the library, every once in a while, to get one of those old film strips of copies of the *Journal* and the *Register*, they go back to the 1800's. He liked to wind his way through them just to see what people were thinking about at such and such a time. And one afternoon he came upon this curious, it was a kind of scandal, about a fellow named Max Pole—M.P.—it jarred Dim's mind. This Max Pole had left town because of gossip that he was keeping unusual company with the wife of a prominent banker. This gave Dim some food for thought, he chewed on it for a while. M.P. must be Max Pole, he figured.

Then one day he was down close to the center of town and there was an old Victorian-type house that was sched-uled for renovation. People renovate everything these days and discover copper domes, for instance, where nobody thought they were. But no matter, Dim saw that the door was open and he walked in. He saw a beautiful stairway with walnut rails and spindles and Dim climbed the stairs, the steps creaking, as they do, and at the top of the stairway there was a huge four-paneled door. Dim stood there, uncertain, but a voice from within said, "Welcome." So Dim turned the knob and the door opened easily and he walked in and there was an old, old man sitting on a bench. The old man raised his arm, he was so old the flesh hung from the bones.

Dim said, "Who are you?"

And the man straightened up because there was pride left in him and said, "Maximus de la Poole."

So this was Max Pole! And Dim said, "Max Pole?" He said, "I have been sent to find you."

And Poole said, "Yes, I have been waiting for you. In fact, do you see the other door shut fast there?"

Dim said, "Yes."

And Maximus de la Poole said, "I have been keeping death waiting on the other side of that door until you came."

Dim was astonished. He said, "I don't know why I was sent, only that a man with blue ice in his eyes asked me to tell you that it was all right."

When Poole heard this, he turned away and Dim understood that this proud man did not want Dim to see the tears starting in his eyes. But when he turned back, Dim saw a man at peace, as if he had received a blessing.

Poole said, "Now I have something for you to take to an old friend. I have this box." And he said, "When you bring her this box, everything will have been completed."

So Dim said, "Well, I'll certainly do my best."

Then Dim took the box and bade Maximus de la Poole good-bye and as Dim shut the door behind him, he heard the other door open.

Well, it wasn't a day or two later in the newspapers, it said that a vagrant had been found inside that house. He was buried in a potter's field. You know there is one, a local field. It has a caretaker, taking care of people who can have no other burial and no kin to see to the last rites. So, Dim figured that was Maximus de la Poole and he brought some flowers out there.

But to go on. Well, at this point, Dim was determined to fulfill his quest, but he wasn't quite sure where he was going with this box. He used to carry it around, he felt a bit stupid and, you know, strange things happened. One time he was on Grand just at the head of Spring when suddenly six or seven cars raced by him and this maniacal laughter came from the drivers' seats. Dim survived that. Another time when he was downtown, suddenly this big headache ball fell and almost crushed him. He looked up and there was a fellow who was demolishing an apartment building. He said, "Boy, wasn't that a close one." Dim felt of course it was a close one, it almost killed him. And another time a brick fell off a building and knocked off his hat. These were just some of his terrifying experiences. It seemed as if every time he was carrying that box, something was trying to do him in.

Finally it was a morning in May and Dim was in this place where the city was going to build a park and there was a little old house in there. It was not, you know, not a big old house like you'd find in a gothic novel or something like that, it was a worker's house. And Dim felt irresistably drawn to it. So he walked up to the door and the wind was blowing against him, trying to keep him out. But he had been attacked by cars and a headache ball and survived, so he wasn't to be put off now.

He went to the front door and the door was open, so he walked in and it was very neat in there. There were no bugs in the corners, as you might have expected. There was no furniture and no curtains. For all practical purposes the house was empty, it seemed like it was abandoned. He went into the parlor and there in a straight-backed chair was a woman with stone-white hair, you know, and a face composed of hundreds and hundreds of wrinkles. She was dressed in a gown that seemed out-sized for her thin, spidery arms. Dim knew that this was the person that he had been destined to meet and so he was not surprised when this lady said to him, "You are Dim, are you not?"

He said, "Yes." And then he noticed above the mantel a portrait in oils of a distinguished man, the very fellow who had been sitting in the back seat of that car at Willemore and Cherry. Dim said, "Your husband?"

The lady nodded her head.

Dim said, "He has a commanding presence."

She said, "To the very bottom of his soul!"

Well, at this point Dim remembered he was holding the

box and he said, "I have this box for you. I was sent by the man in the picture to M.P. and M.P. gave me this box to bring to you."

She took it, you know, but her hands were shaking. Dim had to help her open it. It wasn't tied up, it had a seal he had to break. A box packed with sawdust. And do you know what the woman pulled out of that box? A cut glass champagne goblet with a hollow stem. And as she pulled it out, it glittered in the light. There wasn't much light in the room but whatever was there, the glass seemed to gather it into a kind of melodious composition. Well, the old lady asked Dim to take the goblet into the kitchen and wash it very carefully, which he did. He was proud to do it, he felt proud when he brought it back and gave it to her.

She said, "Now, I have this bottle of special wine and I would like you to share this glass with me."

He opened the wine for her, poured it and it sparkled and bubbled. It was like a burgundy. She put it to her lips and drank some and handed it to Dim and he drank some. And you know as they drank this, handing the glass back and forth, she began to become—Dim could see the burgundy in the stem of the glass, the hollow stem—this most astonishing thing happened. It seemed as if the room was filled with candlelight and this champagne glass was sparkling with the treasured light of the firmament and the old woman before Dim's eyes became extraordinarily beautiful. She had on this lovely gown and she looked like a figure from a book of the hours. She allowed Dim to drink a little more of the gleaming wine and then she took the glass and she drained it.

Then Dim suddenly understood how it could be that one man would expend his life as king to be husband to this woman and another man would spend his entire life honoring her because she had, as she smiled at Dim, she had this unbelievable aura about her, a sense of both helplessness and total command.

She smiled at Dim. "You are a good man," she said, and Dim knew that he would die for her ten times over.

Then she took the last drop of wine and she said, "Oh, poor dear Max." She held the glass out in front of Dim and turned it over. "See, there is no more wine, everything is complete," she said. And her smile was radiant.

At this point Dim just blanked out, he didn't remember anything. A policeman found him wandering around in Iles Park. The policeman sat him down and fanned him—it was a warm May morning—until Dim came somewhat to his senses.

The policeman said, "I think maybe you were a bit light-headed. A little early for a drink, isn't it?"

Dim said, "Well, it would be for beer or something like that."

So the policeman saw to it that Dim got home all right.

Well, you know, Dim would have come back to check that little house out, but that very day some nitwit with a bulldozer came and demolished it, just leveled it, much to everyone's anger in the neighborhood.

The bulldozer operator said, "Well, I have these orders."

It was signed by one of the city officials, but the official in question said he never signed anything. So that's the strange story of Dim's quest. What do you think of that?

The purple martin run

You know, up in Minnesota and South Dakota—well, we have mosquitos, but their mosquitos put dents in the screens all night long. Of course, the natives are used to this, they sleep rather well, but visitors end up tossing restlessly through the night. They think, "What if the screens break and they come in and get us?" So, that's kind of normal in that part of the country, but this one year there were so many mosquitos that when they landed on the trees, the limbs would break under the weight in the tree lots up there. So the town fathers in this one town—it was in Minnesota, just a little bit north of Luverne, you know, where the Sioux quartzite is—they decided to contact Griggsville, Illinois, and get a truckload of purple martins and let them loose in their town to go after the mosquitos. Griggsville is on the other side of the Illinois River—well, if you are on this side, it is—and just west of Valley City. But, no matter.

Now in those days Dim made his living driving a semi. So he got a dispatch from a company in New Berlin to take his White Freightliner over to Griggsville and pick up a load of purple martins. So he did. Well, there was no trouble. The purple martins love people, so all the town fathers over there had to do was line up these coops and the birds flew right in, they wanted to find out what the next adventure would be. And the town fathers loaded them into the truck and shut the gates and Dim took off on his run to Minnesota.

Just inside of Iowa he hit a flash storm. It was so bad he couldn't see and he had to drive up on the shoulder of the road and the wheels got into the mud and he was stuck. There he was when the storm cleared with this truckload of purple martins. But, luckily, a troop of Girl Scouts came walking down the highway and they all had these ash poles, walking sticks. They really didn't need them, but those poles are what they wanted to have at that particular time and they were swinging them around and having sword fights with them. So, they came over to see if they could help Dim out.

Dim thought about what to do and he said, "Okay, girls, when I sound the horn, you hit the side of the truck with those walking sticks of yours."

And when they got all set, he sounded the horn and they hit the truck. And when they hit the truck, he hit the pedal and he got out of there because, you see, when the martins heard that noise, they all flew up from their perches.

Now you have to understand that this isn't a folk tale like the one they tell in Grand Tower, Illinois, about the slow raise in the railroad tracks down there and the long freights. Well, there's one crossing where they can barely get the cars over and they have the brakeman stand out there with a big stick and he hits every fourth car, which is filled with hummingbirds, and the hummingbirds fly up and that raises the car up and the effort of the humming-birds is just enough to get that freight rolling towards Chester.

What really happened in Iowa was—and Dim had calculated this—when the Girl Scouts hit the side of the White Freightliner, the martins left their perches and this took the weight off, but the birds didn't raise the truck. It was just the weight lifted off the perches that enabled Dim to pull out of the mud he was in. So, he got up to Minne-sota and the town had a big festival and the martins ate up most of the mosquitos that year.

Of course, they had to return them in the fall. Otherwise Griggsville wouldn't have any purple martins left, handing them out to everybody like that.

Dim's strange wedding

This is about when Dim went to Rock Island and Moline and to Augustana College, where he saw the Bibles. One of the Bibles was open, but Dim couldn't read it because it was a German Bible in old script. However, he did recognize that it was opened to the Psalms. Dim appreciated that. He wanted to see some eagles, too, but they probably wouldn't have been there anyway because eagles generally horse around up there in the Mississippi valley during the winter months. This was in the summer, a very hot and sultry day, one of those summer days that we are experiencing this summer where if you have a deep thought, you break out in a sweat.

So it was a long day for Dim and he was driving around and at about seven o'clock in the early evening he came to a church. There were cars in front of the church and it was a Saturday and he thought, "Well, they are probably having a service" and even more to the point, the service was probably air conditioned. So he thought he'd stop in and profit spiritually as well as corporeally. Dim liked words like "corporeally."

Well, he had something to learn about this particular church. The pastor of it had spent his whole clerical life terrorizing the congregation. This man could shoot a dart of indignation out of his eye at a particular parishioner who might have been talking or nodding during a service, you know, and it would hit him right in the solar plexus like a spear. A man hit like that wouldn't be able to walk straight for a week. This pastor savagely enjoyed occasions like funerals and baptisms and weddings—though with a baptism he was always frustrated because the infant knew nothing about his indignation and was either crying or asleep and with the funerals the center of attention there didn't care anymore what the pastor did. But when there was a wedding, everybody was present and on edge and on these occasions this man was in his heaven, so to speak. He harried them all—the bride, the groom, the girl who was to sing "O Promise Me," the little tykes who carried baskets of flowers, even the parents and grandparents, everyone there. They all had to proceed according to the numbers or be killed. And he would—he had this idea that a wedding should be like a cabbage, all smooth around the outside. Everybody was afraid of, you know, committing a boo-boo and denting the pastor's cabbage or something. So at the moment Dim was getting out of his car, the people in church were smiling at one another paralyzed with fear.

Well, the groom was standing in front of the church—there was a little time before the wedding was to begin—when suddenly a car roared up as Dim was about to enter the church. This car was driven by a Western Union messenger and he gave the message to the groom, who opened it up and read, "Family crisis. Return at once to Dallas. Urgent."

The groom cried, "Oh, oh, what is happening, what is happening?" and he looked at his watch and said, "Oh, I have to get married!" and "Oh, there is a plane going out, but I would have to go a hundred miles an hour to catch it!" and the Western Union messenger cried, "It's all right. I'll take you in the company car."

Then the groom saw Dim and his eyes lit up. He thrust the message into Dim's hand, saying, "Take care of everything, will you?" And he took off his coat and he said, "Here, put this on" and pushed Dim into the church. Then he drove off with the Western Union man.

Well, Dim was looking all around, blinking in the light, and everybody in the church was whispering, "Hurry up, hurry up! You're already late. You want us all to be killed?"

So Dim, not knowing what else to do, went down the aisle. Now the congregation—these people weren't stupid, they realized that Dim wasn't the real groom, you understand, and they knew he was coming from the back of the church when he should have been over at the side altar. But he had on the groom's coat and boutonniere and that was enough for them. They knew it was a terrible breach of decorum because the bride was already up there, but they said to each other, "Better him than us."

Well, Dim went up there. What else could he have done? And he missed every cue. For instance, the pastor had told the groom when it was time to kiss the bride, "You stand there and you look at her with great intensity and count to seven and then you kiss her." Well, Dim didn't know anything about counting to seven. He just kissed her any way he could.

The pastor was seething and the congregation was trying to scrunch down below pew level, each person expecting a terrible bolt. Anyway, you know, there was a stone angel at the back of the church who appeared to be smiling and when that pastor hit the poor creature in the stomach with one of his indignation darts, he left that angel with its cheeks puffed out in an expression of absolute piety.

The wedding party left the church as quickly as possible after the pastor had stormed out of the sanctuary. They hustled into their cars and off to the reception. Everybody was smiling and teary eyed and touching Dim on the shoulders and arms and rejoicing and thanking him for saving them during the wedding. The bride and the bride's parents were off with Dim in a happy dream.

By then, they had gotten a message from the groom, of course. Now let me tell you what happened. The groom's family was one of two in Dallas by that name and it was the other family that had the crisis. The groom had rushed back to Texas, but there was no problem. It was just that a cousin of his had sent the message to Illinois, thinking it was him.

Anyway, the groom came back that night on an owl flight and the next day they said, "Look, we don't want to go back into that church." So they went to the city hall and Dim came as a witness. The wedding party was so happy the wedding had been rescued that no one complained about waiting in line. There were all kinds of people ahead of them with bruised arms and black eyes being attended to in court, but finally the party got up there and the marriage was performed. And then the bride and groom invited everybody present to a big reception. And you know one of the interesting things that happened? Some of those people were so inspired by this marriage that was obviously heaven sent, that several of them reformed and got married themselves and lived happily ever after.

Well, Dim, after all this had taken place, drove back home. He drove up the Rock River valley and it was a lovely afternoon and he turned south on Highway 74 and began to climb up the hills toward Galesburg. And you know what occurred to him? The lines from the Psalms about the sparrow that found herself a house and the swallow a nest for herself where she has lain her young. And Dim was suddenly, idiotically happy driving south on I-74. So that's the story about the strange wedding in the Quad Cities.

The wedding night? Oh, the folks were all partying and they knew that Dim wasn't the regular groom. I guess I left an important part out of the story. But this reminds me of Dim's curious statement that he, too, in his day had been one of those wonderful monogamous males who cavorted and bugled in the meadows of love. Of course, I don't know myself whether he is referring to the Quad Cities incident or whether he really had an earlier marriage that I don't know anything about.

Some Dim proverbs

Because of the popularity of Dim's proverbs I wish to include here most of the ones he left scattered throughout his notebooks. There were not as many as I would have supposed, which prompts me to speculate that the vast majority of Dim's wise sayings are in oral tradition. Certainly this is true for some of the most well-known of them. For instance, "The best nails have average heads" has no counterpart in the notes. Be this as it may, here are the ones that I have collected:

> The goat in the onion rows considers the joys of a democratic society.

> When elephants mate, it rains in 30 days.

> The tortoise did not know it was in a race, this is the advantage of being hatched from an egg.

> One sick frog inspires another.

> The hen that lays a square egg will not cluck cluck.

> The forgetful elephant is never remembered.

> A slow sundown will lick its own plate clean.

Before going to bed, box six or seven rounds with a friend.

Ten watermelons feel more confident than two watermelons.

When the mouse married the weasel, the other mice wanted to know did he like cheese for breakfast?

The first drops of rain observe the speed limit.

When two follows one, three is disconsolate.

The mouse that can swallow the golf tee can putt the cat.

Two right shoes will assume there are not any others.

The pick handle never feels strong enough to go it alone.

The man with an alert mind thinks of something every day.

If a telephone rings three times, there may be something wrong with it.

When you paint yourself into a corner, go out and buy a new brush.

The man with nothing more to lose will gamble the moonlight.

Thirty days hath September, things do not change very much.

There is nothing extraordinary in the subject matter, certainly, but some of us here in central Illinois have taken Dim's saws to heart and accepted them as rules for the proper conduct of our lives.

The five-mile worm

It seems that Dim was looking around in his pantry one
day and he found this plastic bag full of dehydrated mushrooms and he remembered that he had bought them at a
local grocery and they were a Japanese kind of mushroom.
If you crumble one of them into an omelet or something
every day, it reduces your cholesterol about 70 percent.
Dim thought, well, it was time for him to reduce his cholesterol, so he decided he would make a mushroom soufflé.
First he crumbled up the mushrooms and then he got some
eggs and flour and milk, and he mixed it all up and put it
in the oven. It rose up and made this beautiful mushroom-
like mushroom soufflé. And then he decided because it was
summer he'd go out on the side porch and eat it.

He was all ready to put the fork in when the phone
rang. It was his Aunt Matilda from Utah, I think she was
from Provo, Utah. Aunt Matilda only called once in a
hundred years, you know, but she wanted to catch up on
the family, what happened to the Softlights and the Dims
and everybody. Dim's mother was a Softlight, he was
related on his mother's side. While he was giving Aunt
Matilda the rhyme and reasons of all the family in Illinois
and hither and thither—and that took a good long time—

well, anyway, by the time she hung up the phone and Dim went out, a bunch of earthworms had gotten into the soufflé and eaten it all.

Dim didn't think much about this except that somehow or other nature had cheated him out of a soufflé. But he was a tender-hearted man, he wasn't going to get angry with the worms because they had gone after his mushrooms. The next day he decided to do the same thing and he baked another soufflé and like the first one it was perfectly beautiful, a curvaceous creation. Ah. And he brought it out on the side porch again and, you know, the phone rang again and this time it was Aunt Charlotte from Greensboro, North Carolina. Aunt Charlotte and Aunt Matilda were twins, so anything that Matilda did, Charlotte would get waves. And Charlotte wanted to check up on everything that Dim had told Matilda. By the time he got through telling Aunt Charlotte everything he had told Aunt Matilda and she had commented on everything Aunt Matilda had told him, he went out on the porch and lo the worms had gotten into the soufflé again. Dim didn't know whether it was his eyes or what, but they appeared to be a little larger than they had been the day before.

Well, the next day he wasn't about to make another soufflé and have some aunt he had never heard of call to check on the other two and repeat the whole thing over again. So he just decided he'd go out on the side porch and relax, and you know what? All the worms were sticking their little heads up and they were all watching the side porch. The whole yard was full of these worms like little periscopes and they were waiting for him to bring out another soufflé. That's the truth. So Dim, was he going to frustrate the multitude of lumbricus terrestris, or whatever they're called? No. He just went and made another soufflé and they jumped right in.

I don't want to make a whole evening of this, but those powdered mushrooms had a curious effect and Dim's first intuition was correct. The worms got larger. In fact it wasn't but a day or so when he had several that were large enough to repair the spring on his screen door. It broke and he didn't have time to go up to the hardware and get it fixed, so he just hitched a couple of them together. They were amiable, they'd pull the screen shut when he opened it until they got tired and then he'd have to replace them with a couple of others. And, you know, he had trouble with pigeons up in the eaves of his house. Well, he got a forked stick and the worms just stretched themselves across it and he used them for sling shots. He shot out the pigeons with pebbles, using the worms. I don't want to belabor this, but some of those worms grew rather large, at least three or four feet, enough to give a blacksnake pause.

Now all these worms, they didn't bother the townspeople, Dim's neighbors, except there was one extraordinary thing and I want to hasten to that in order not to prolong this story. One worm grew by geometric progression. It doubled its length every day and by the time it became, you know, worrisome, they had a city council—have you ever seen a city council operate, trying to decide what to do? By the time they had argued back and forth what to do about this worm that was getting bigger and bigger, the worm stretched from the east end of town all the way to I-55, by the truck stop there. The thing was over five miles long. What do you think of that?

I tell you it caused problems, but no one could say anything because by the time it was five miles long, it was declared a national treasure. The county supervisor had to come out and jack it up over Sugar Creek and over the county roads, but for the kids it was wonderful because they used it as a bicycle path. They would bicycle out to the truck stop and get a sodie, you know (sodie we call it out here), and then they'd turn around and come back to town. Well, the worm excited considerable interest and now the story takes a ghoulish turn. I don't know how long earthworms live, I'd have to check that up with authorities at the university, but this one became internationally famous. No one would, they couldn't, put it in a zoo or something, a five-mile-long worm, so they waited for it to die. And after awhile it wasn't moving, so they figured it was dead and then they came and sliced it all up and there was international cooperation. The Russians came and the Chinese, everybody. What they wanted to see was what it was that made the worm grow so long. Yes. Because it could have revolutionary consequences for agriculture. A thing like that could level whole mountains, not to mention what you could manage if you could learn how to eat it.

They ran countless experiments on the bits and pieces, but all they ever found out was that it was just like any other earthworm, only it was bigger.

At that point they went back to Dim to find out what he knew about the mushrooms, but by then they were all gone and he said, "Well, it was just those Japanese mushrooms I bought." So they all went out and got those mushrooms and everybody enjoyed them in omelets as you would expect, but no worm ever ate any. They weren't interested in them. And then one day Dim was looking at the container his original mushrooms came in and he saw there was a little piece of paper at the bottom of it. He thought it was in Japanese, but when he brought it out under the light, it said Thackers Gap. Thackers Gap? That's down below Harrisburg and it's up about, oh, seven miles from Shawneetown. A lot of Eastern Band Shawnee still live around there, they never left.

So the scientists went down there because they figured it must have been a special variety of mushroom that is grown around Thackers Gap and is marketed. But the Shawnee said they didn't know, they had heard about things used in peyote cults people would take to have visions, but they had never heard about a mushroom that could extend a worm. In fact they were humorous about it, you know, all those people up north in the state trying to get mushrooms to grow worms. And so the conclusion was finally reached that whatever Dim had, it must have been local mushrooms, but it was a mutated strain and he was the only one that had them and the worms got those and it affected them all, but there was a severe mutation in that one worm that grew to be five miles long.

So that's the story about the worms and the mushrooms. Dim was very lucky his aunts kept calling. Maybe those two old twin aunts knew something and they were trying to protect Dim from some kind of terrible fate. What if he had grown 15 miles high? He would have been embarrassed, don't you think?

The Hannibal frogs

Well, you know Dim had a fascination for the historical and the picturesque. So he went over to Hannibal and the first thing he did, he went down south of there and toured the cave where Tom Sawyer and Becky Thatcher got lost. He went with a group, they had those electric torches, you know, and they got to a certain spot and the guide flashed up on the wall. He said, "You see that name? Well, a grandchild of the man who wrote that name was in this cave and saw it and recognized it. And she was so taken with it that she had her wedding right here on this spot under the name." Then the guide said, "You might say the marriage got off to a rocky start." He said that.

And then someone else said, "Well, I hope that marriage didn't cave in on them."

So Dim endured this and watched a couple of bats flying around.

Then on the way back towards Hannibal, Dim went up on this precipice called Lovers Leap. And he got a spectacular view of the river, especially north. He could see all of Hannibal and all up the Mississippi valley. Beautiful. So while he was there someone said, "Do you suppose anybody ever did leap off this cliff?"

And another fellow from the town said, "Well yes, everybody was leaping off of it during the Depression." He said, "They lined up and they paid the city of Hannibal a quarter apiece to jump off. That's the way the city government kept going."

And Dim began to think, "Everybody wants to tell a big story in this town."

Well, then he went into Hannibal to have some lunch and there were three or four of the old town guys trying to convince a woman at the next table that they had these handmade cigars in Hannibal—you know, back before 1900—and they really made them out of paper with just a Havana wrap, but they were so good that the cigars sold in Chicago as genuine Havanas. People were smoking Hannibal newspapers in Chicago the old men were telling the woman. Can you imagine that? I mean this was Dim's day.

So he wandered town a little and then he came to a point on the river. It had steel pilings there to hold the bank up, a place for boats to come in. And there was an old fellow sitting there. Of course, Dim was always affable. So he felt that if he were sharing the point with this old man, he should relate. And he said, "How are you?"

And the old man said, "Well, I'm fine." He said, "I always like it out here on the point." And, "Are you enjoying the town?"

And Dim said, "Yes, I've been to Mark Twain's home and here and there."

The old man looked at him and said, "Clemens. We always called him Clemens. Sam Clemens."

Dim was startled a little, so he said, "Twain, Clemens, whatever. Everybody in this town thinks they can stand straight up and tell a big lie."

"Well," the old man said, "as to that, I'm going to tell you something about Sam Clemens and others from around here. They didn't go from this valley and learn to be what they were. They had everything they needed right here." The old man straightened up. "Take Floyd Dell and Susan Glaspell and George Cram Cook up in the Quad Cities area."

Dim didn't know who those people were, but he wanted to be polite and so he said, "Oh, yes."

Well, with that the old man warmed to his argument. "Now take Clemens," he said. "When he was here, he was just a little fellow and, you know, they had a frog here." He said, "This frog had a peculiar name, probably because some child was trying to say something else. The frog's name was Evie Lovey. Everybody liked him. What this frog could do is, he could leap across the Mississippi River. There was a place out there in those days called Glasscock Island and he would have to bounce off of that if the wind wasn't strong enough. He would just hit with his—well, you know how frogs go. And that would get him right on the other side and then he would leap back. Of course, he would have to sort of tack in the wind, but he would get across again—and that river is really wide there, it's not narrow like it is in front of St. Louis. Huge, huge stream. Yes. And this frog could do that. He could leap all the way across and back. And that was Evie Lovey."

Well, Dim thought, "All right, I can tolerate this."

Then the old man said, "Yes, and you know there was another frog. His name was Calvin Neverest."

Dim said, "Was he a Presbyterian of some kind?" He was being a little witty.

But the old man was very serious. He said, "Not that anybody ever knew. He never professed. Of course, he might have turned up in church in a boy's pocket, but he never showed any signs of piety. And the thing was, this frog only jumped off of Lovers Leap up there." The old man said, "You know about Lovers Leap?"

Dim said, "Yes." He was getting a little exasperated. "Yes I do," he bit off.

"So anyway," the old man went on, "Cal Neverest would leap off Lovers Leap and land over on the other side, just flop there. And the kids like little Sam—we always called him Sam—they'd get a skiff and go over and bring him back and then they'd bring him up to Lovers Leap and he would jump across again. It was some kind of game this frog liked."

Dim went along with this, not wanting to offend the old man. Dim figured he had been out in the heat too long. The old man said, "The other frog, though, Evie Lovey, he had some unfortunate things happen. He leaped back into the middle of a family reunion once and squashed a whole platter of deviled eggs. And another time he landed on the mourners bench when there was a revival meeting. Disturbed everybody because it happened while the preacher was talking about the plagues of Egypt. So it was determined— what can you do with a frog? They were going to send him to the happy hopping ground, if you know what I mean. But they came upon this wonderful solution. In order to prevent Evie from making those leaps anymore, they fed him buckshot so he'd just hop around on the point. The way they did this, they pasted small paper wings on each one of the shots and bounced them up in the air so that Evie thought they were real flies. Evie never knew the difference. And he wasn't sad about not being able to jump across the river anymore because people always came down and petted him and fed him whatever bugs were handy. That's how they stopped him from being a nuisance."

Dim was just sitting there, you know, astonished, and wishing that he were somewhere else.

Then the old man said, "See, when Sam Clemens left here he already had everything he needed for that gambling story he wrote."

Well, Dim—it was a hot day and he became a little testy. He said, "That is really a lot of baloney and it's an ill-told story. I mean, if you're going to talk about Mark Twain, you ought at least to be a better storyteller."

The old man was taken back, just kept looking at Dim with a wounded expression.

Dim said, "Frogs jumping across the Mississippi. How could you expect me to believe that?"

At that very moment while Dim was waxing righteous, this black dot came soaring out of the sky from the east and got larger and larger until you could see it was a good-sized frog. It plopped right down in front of the two of them and shook itself off like an Airedale. The old man smiled and patted the frog's head. Dim was just staring speechless.

And then the frog said "Nedep! Nedep!"

And the old man turned and nudged Dim in the ribs as if Dim were in on some kind of conspiracy. He said, "This frog reports the depth of the water. The only trouble is, it doesn't matter whether we're in a drought or the whole bottom for six miles over there is in flood 40 feet deep. This frog always comes back and says, `Nedep! Nedep!' He's good-natured, but he's not very bright."

Dim finally found his voice. He said, "Ah, oh, I don't know what to say."

The old man said, "That's all right. This frog's the one we call Hannibal Pete." Then he opened his big fishing creel and the frog hopped in and the old man closed it and got up and walked away.

So Dim drove back from Hannibal that afternoon. He drove fast through Pittsfield, John Hay's town, and Carlinville where Mary Austin used to live. He was a sadder and a wiser man. You could say that.

The Cuba mushroom mine

This is about the time Dim came back from Galesburg and he stopped in Cuba, Illinois. Cuba once advertized itself as the strip mining capital of the world, that's the truth, I remember seeing that. Anyway, that area up there is full of strip mines and reclaimed land. Well, it was late at night and Dim was a bit thirsty, so he thought he'd get something to drink, you know, but what's open in a country town at night but a bar?

So he went in and this place was full of people who were just sitting around looking exasperated. Men would pick up their drinks and then look incredulous and set their drinks down again. It was an amazing thing to see, all these people, just sitting there shaking their heads. Well, Dim wanted to know what this was all about and they were not unfriendly, so they told him.

It seems that one of the neighbors there ran a family business in strip mining. His name was Rod Scoop, Dim said. I think that's what it was. And as you know, according to the law when you are going to strip-mine, you have to take all the soil up and put it somewhere. You take up that A-horizon, which is the dark loam, the black soil, and you put that in one place and then you take the B-horizon, and that's the clay, and you put that in another place and then the C-horizon contains pebbles, you know, and sand and detritus, stuff like that, and then you get down to where the coal is.

Well, Scoop did that. He scooped up the A- B- C-horizons and then he strip-mined 120 acres of his grand-mother's deeded land, from a Van Buren land grant, and made a profit on the coal.

"And do you know what the dummy did?" the people in the bar asked Dim. "He put the A-horizon back first and then the B-horizon and then the C-Horizon. Everything was upside down. Can you imagine a man that stupid?" That's what they were saying in the bar.

Now this had happened some time ago. The towns-people would run out there and throw their garbage on it and try to compost it. They'd rake their leaves over there, but nothing helped. It was a disaster.

Well, Dim was there and, you know, he was not unlike the Wizard of Oz, or maybe Mighty Mouse. He thought awhile and he said, "That loam is down there where the coal was?"

And they said, "Yes."

"Well," he said, "If you make an entrance and go down something like—what is it?—48 inches, so that you're just under that loam, and you make a tunnel straight across and then you tack a very fine wire mesh up under the roof of the tunnel, I just happen to be bringing back from Galesburg the spores of a very interesting new mushroom."

And, you know, those people all went out and did just that. And they planted—all they had to do was take a paper sack full of spores and an electric fan and shake the spores out in front of it and it blew them all up onto this rich loam. Remember, that A-horizon was lying right on top of Dim's wire mesh along with the compost or anything else that had leached down from above. It made for a bumper crop of mushrooms. They grew down through the wire and you could sweep big swaths of them off with knives and they'd just grow again. Or you could pick them one by one and get the root, too. Some people thought the root was particularly delicious in their pastries.

Well, they did that and everybody wanted to buy these mushrooms, you know. Store-bought mushrooms are not cheap, so these were a bargain. There's a curious side to this, those mushrooms wouldn't grow anywhere else, just where the soil had been upside down. So Scoop's mistake ended up rather happily because of the sympathy of Dim for this fellow Scoop and his family.

The Sugar Creek mud turtles

Well, we get extremes of weather here, you know, and Dim had an experience in one of those terrible drought years where you had almost no rain in the summer. At that time Sugar Creek pretty much dried up, except for a string of water holes from about the middle of Lake Springfield on back south of Auburn to the other side of the golf course. People used to come out and dig into those water holes to get carp and various other kinds of fish, some that they had never seen before. Well, Dim and two of his friends went down to the creek to look the situation over. And one of the friends when he went to the edge of the water hole where they were, he saw a mud turtle with its two feet sticking out, just there on the bank. So he got a stick and poked at the turtle and the turtle grabbed ahold of it, as they do, and then Dim's friend began to pull out with both hands. But the turtle dug its feet into the bank against him, so Dim's other friend went down there and then Dim helped too and the three of them pulled this turtle out.

But what they learned was that if one mud turtle gets in trouble that way, another mud turtle will come up and grab ahold of the tail of the one in trouble. So the first thing you know they were trying to drag two turtles out and then three turtles. And this went on most of the morning until finally they had dragged a hundred yards of mud turtles out of that pond. Well, they were exhausted, as you could guess, and they ended up lying out there on the shoulder of the road below the old pioneer cemetery, just staring at the sky. That's one hundred yards of mud turtles. Well, just, you know, to put this into mathematical perspective, if you had three mud turtles to the yard, that would be 300 mud turtles and if each mud turtle weighed 10 pounds, that would be, what? Three thousand pounds of mud turtles. That's a ton and a half, a short ton that is. So it was no wonder they were too exhausted even to get up when those turtles all made a 180-degree turn and each turtle grabbed onto the tail of the turtle that had been behind him and they all went back into their water hole in Sugar Creek. It was the greatest loss of turtle soup there ever was, Dim said, but he and his friends were too tired to get up and do anything about it.

Dim's catalog of dust

Well, this is what Dim calls a catalog of dust. That's his very phrase and it's an account of things that took place when they had a summer without much rain. It got into the very late summer and by then the dust was so thick on the ground that the worms began to cough. You could hear them, you know—eugh eugh eugh eugh! That's how they sounded. And when the robins would get out and cock their heads over to hear, they would become unbalanced. They had no footing and they'd sink right down into the ground. Dim managed to save a lot of the birds using a plastic sink strainer. It was just large enough so he could scoop them out of the dust as they disappeared. It was so dry that once at sundown Dim saw an owl swoop down on a toad and when the owl struck, the toad broke into 40 pieces. It was about that time that corn began popping in the shucks, right there on the stalks, and it was dangerous to go out in the fields.

Well, it wasn't long after this that big cracks opened in the earth, especially up around the VFW hall, and when the cracks got deep enough, they exposed an abandoned mine. Now there weren't supposed to be any mines under the town, you know. They all went east toward the highway, but there was one there. And, well, it was a good thing because they put ladders down and people would go there to keep cool. They were able to save on the air conditioners that way. At first they'd just go down there and sit around reading magazines, but after a while the members of the VFW started a 24-hour bingo game. It kept everybody busy and it was a sort of cheerful thing, everybody playing bingo in the mine while escaping the heat. And it was a good thing, too, for the VFW because the veterans were able to put a new roof on their hall and replace the old galvanized water pipes with copper. And Dim bingo'd three times in one shaft down there that summer himself.

Well, it was so dry and hot that up by the big highway where the oil wells are, they began pumping graphite. There was a dark haze all over that particular intersection. But, you know, at the country club the grounds keepers were furious because the deer would put their triangle prints deep into the greens. You see, when every grass plot in town was brown and dry, the golf course greens were lush and watered. The deer came there to lick the wet grass.

Well, one morning just before dawn Dim was up there collecting golf balls. The players slice and hook the balls across the road into a field opposite the golf course and Dim was over there collecting a bag of golf balls for his nephew, who was going into, as Dim said, the pedestrian sport. Anyway, Dim had just come back on the road and you know what he saw? He saw the Mouse King come with all the mice and they gathered around the little deer prints that were filled with water and they all drank there. Dim said it was one of the most beautiful things that he'd ever seen in nature. So that's the story of the catalog of dust.

Sheep production

Well, you remember there used to be quite a number of
sheep raised in Illinois. But in time it got too expensive to
raise sheep. The price of mutton and lamb wasn't worth it
finally. Well now, there is a story in back of that. It seems
like there was a fellow who had a lot of sheep near
Palmyra and he was telling Dim that he'd like to increase
his production. So Dim consulted around and figured that if
you fed these sheep on various herbs and weeds and
whatnot that were available, you wouldn't have to pay for
the fodder. They grow all over Illinois and if you had the
right combination, you might get an extremely rich mixture
for the sheep. This included dock and creeping charlie, fox
tail and lambs quarters, buttonweed, that sort of thing.

So the fellow in Palmyra fed the sheep on this and they
quadrupled. Well, the word got out and everybody did the
same thing and suddenly you had sheep all over Illinois.
The market just collapsed. That's what happened. It hasn't
really recovered yet. It's just the last couple of years people
have begun to raise more sheep. Now as you think about
this particular story, I'll explain a wonderful thing in it. You
know, if they had just tripled, there wouldn't be anything
special to remark on. But they quadrupled and Dim

thought that this was because of some combination of the weeds with the lambs quarters. There is no way of telling now because Dim left his formula in his shirt pocket at the laundromat, I think it was the Rainbow Wash House in Virden, and the detergent cleaned the ink right off the back of the envelope he had it written on.

Dim and the floating sheep

There's a little story that follows on the sheep raising venture Dim had a part in. I can preface this by saying that Dim had read an account of sheep in Arabia written by an old Greek author. The Arabians told this author that they had sheep there with long, heavy tails and they had to build little carts to attach to the sheep because their tails were so heavy, they couldn't drag themselves along without some support. Dim figured this was just some folk story or the Arabians were putting the Greek on. But then he got a call from a fellow over by Waverly, who told him that he had these sheep with huge tails and the same thing was happening. Dim was amazed.

So he went over to see what he could do and he figured that making carts for them was just too expensive, considering the cost of wheels and labor and everything. What he did was he got some balloons and filled them with gas and attached them to the tails of the sheep and this kept the tails up, so everybody was happy. But the first time he did it, he attached too many balloons and the poor animal flew up in the air and they had the devil of a time trying to get it down. Fortunately it got caught in a tree just this side of Jacksonville, so it didn't soar up into the atmosphere.

Well, the word about the flying sheep got around and, you know, there were some people, local people, too, who thought it might be a good idea to have these sheep up in the air so that they could have a kind of sheep skeet shoot. But that was met with distaste by other people in the area. People were thinking, "Why, these sheep will be falling into our gardens and ruining our rows of beans and flattening the rhubarb." Preachers got up in the pulpit, also, and had all kinds of nasty things to say. So, as far as anybody knows it was only the one sheep that flew to Jacksonville.

The Olmec head

Dim was up on Sugar Creek in late June one time. He
wanted to visit a hole a real estate developer had dug
supposing that a lake would come of it and attract some
homeowners. But there wasn't enough water in it to make
a toad feel comfortable, so Dim was there hoping to find
an arrowhead or a flint drill in the rubble. And it was hot,
so he sat down and as you will when there is dust handy,
trailed his fingers through the dirt.

That is how he discovered the green stone, the big
stone. Around in this country there are no big stones, there
aren't even any small stones to speak of, just deep prairie
gumbo. Limestone had to be carted in for the six or seven
houses in the town that have hewn stone basements.
Anyway, Dim pushed the dirt from around the green stone,
but that is not right. What really happened was the more he
uncovered, the more there was of the stone to be seen.
How about that?

So he went back to town and got several of his friends
and they brought picks and spades and began digging
around the stone. It took many days to do it, but finally
they had cleared about 10 feet down on all sides and they
knew they had come on the archaeological find of the

century, that there was nothing like this in North America. The nearest to it, probably, are the big heads, the heads that are found in southern Mexico and in Central American countries. They look a little like Joe Louis, the famous boxer everybody used to hear in matches over the radio in the thirties.

Well, they were going to get a big crane and try to winch that head out of the Sugar Creek development and it was just at sundown on the Fourth of July when they finally got the crane in place, had it all ready to do the job. Now at this moment Dim had to relieve himself and he was too modest to be seen standing against a bush, so he went across the road and behind a shed there.

While he was gone, an extraordinary thing happened. The green stone head began to fracture into a million pieces and a vague mist spread across the meadows and, you know, all the people standing around fell into a deep trance. They seemed to be poured into position like the old lead soldiers children used to collect into armies during the Great Depression. All this happened very quickly and when Dim came back, the mist had vanished, but everyone was still asleep. So it turned out that he was the only one who saw millions of ebony sylphs with silver wings fretted with gold, soaring from the fragments of the green head into the timber along Sugar Creek. Millions of little lights, Dim said, so beautiful he was stunned watching them.

That is the story as Dim figured it out. When the others woke up, they didn't remember anything, they had no recollection at all of a green stone head and no idea why a big crane was standing over an empty hole in a field above Sugar Creek south of town. Dim was left alone to wonder at what he had seen, but he was lucky enough to find a small piece of the green stone, the only thing left to prove that the great head had been there. So he took it home and put it on his mantel. Sometimes in the years that followed, when it was The Fourth of July and just at sundown, Dim could have sworn that the little piece of stone on his mantel emitted a faint glow, but he was never quite sure, only a little giddy remembering what he had witnessed once.

Tapper

You may have read somewhere that they think now that
the child in the womb is able to learn and respond to
something. Well, there was an uncle of Dim's. This uncle's
wife was pregnant and he was very patriotic. He was called
Boston Massacre Dim locally. Anyway, he had been in the
First World War and he had been a radio operator, so he
knew Morse code and he started out very simply by sort of
tapping his wife's stomach. And, you know, the little tyke
in there responded immediately. He would kick at the spot
where Dim's uncle was tapping. And then the uncle would
tap over on the other side and the little fellow would kick
there, too. And so after a while the uncle started tapping
"Hi, baby." Well, you can imagine, it was really a day of
rejoicing when after about a week the baby tapped back,
"Hi." He didn't—the baby didn't know who it was he was
talking to. That's why he didn't say "Boston Massacre" or
"Father."

Well, Dim's uncle immediately went to work because
he wanted the baby to be as patriotic as he was. He began
tapping out the "Star Spangled Banner" and the baby would
tap back. I tell you the uncle, Boston Massacre Dim, got the
song all the way—let's see, how far did he get? He got all

the way to "the land of the free" and his wife went into labor. Can you imagine that? He had the anthem almost completed. And the baby was born and he was crying and crying and squalling, and Boston Massacre tapped on his little hand, "Hi, baby," and do you know what that baby did? He tapped back, "and the home of the brave." Well, that was something, the completed "Star Spangled Banner" by a child one hour old.

What happened after that was, the child and the father never spoke together. They just tapped back and forth. It drove the old lady wild. And the only time they really communicated verbally was, say, when the father was upstairs in the bedroom and the son was down in the basement with a jigsaw or something and he'd send a message by way of his mother that he'd like five bucks to go out, he had a date, see. And the mother would go upstairs and say, "Massacre, Tapper wants five dollars."

And the father would say, "Well, I've got four and a quarter."

And she'd go down and say, "How about four and a quarter?"

And he'd say, "Oh, that's fine. Tell Pop thanks."

And that's the only time they communicated. So that's the story of Boston Massacre Dim and his child, Tapper, as he was called.

The Lake Springfield rat float

Dim was a rather curious fellow and one time he went up
to the university to watch an experiment with rats. In this
experiment they have one group of rats that swim around
in a big tub of water. This group of rats is compared with
another group of rats. These other rats don't do anything
except sit around in their cages and eat lettuce. After a
while, they check these unhealthy ones against the healthy
rats that swim in the tub. See how their hearts are doing,
and whatever.

Now what fascinated Dim was that the old and experi-
enced rats didn't swim. They just hung below the surface of
the water with only the tips of their noses sticking out. So
the university always had to have somebody watching the
tub and poking those lazy rats with a stick to keep the
experiment valid. That's the only way they could make the
old rats do their duty.

Well, Dim was amazed and he thought maybe he could
learn to float like that. So one time when he was at Lake
Springfield, he went swimming out toward the—what is it
called?—the dike. Yes, he was out there in the deep water,
so he just abandoned himself and managed to float with his
arms and legs dangling down and just his nose and eyes

out of the water. The first time he did it people thought he was drowning or something, but after a while they got used to it.

And, you know, some of the fellows who liked to swim at the lake learned to do that just the way Dim did. These were big guys. They had huge arms that didn't hang down straight and stomachs that overpowered their swimming trunks. They had little children following them around you wouldn't believe were theirs because the kids were so small. And they had tattoos on their arms that said "Death before Dishonor" or "Laura" in blue hearts or "Mother." There were about 10 or 15 of these fellows and they'd swim out and float around like that with just their eyes and noses out of the water.

That was all right, except that one day some New Yorkers, who weren't used to Lake Springfield, happened by and decided they would take a swim at the public beach. They swam right out into the deep water and almost had a heart attack. They didn't know what it was out there, a bunch of alligators or maybe hippos or some other strange hard-hat predator. Well, things didn't turn out too badly. The guards got them in and started their hearts and everything, you know, pumped the water out of them and explained to them that it was just the fellows floating around dimly in the lake, so to speak. Well, those New Yorkers left and never did come back. Never came back to Springfield either, Dim said.

The French-intensive method

There is another story that goes along with the rat-float story. You know, there is a lot of silt in that Lake Springfield water and one year the beach authorities decided to turn off the hot showers in order to economize. At this point people who used to take showers decided they wouldn't take these cold showers, and Dim was among them. When he came home, though, he clogged up the drains taking a shower there. It was all that Lake Springfield dirt coming off. So he invented what he called his French-intensive method. He just made this little portable shower that he could put over this or that spot in his garden. Then every time he came back from the lake, he'd wash about a pound and a half of really rich soil into his plot. Well, that was the year things started going bad at Fiat Allis and what he was doing attracted a lot of people who only had marginal work that summer. These people took Dim's method seriously and they grew all sorts of things. They grew radishes from that Lake Springfield mud that were three feet long. They used to call them tyrannosaurus radishes to distinguish them from the smaller horseradishes. That's what Dim said anyway.

The vegetarians

Well, this town was over there on the other side of Lowder and it was called I-don't-know-where-it-is, Illinois. That's the truth, I don't make these things up, it's all written in Dim's notebooks. The way you got to it, you went to Lowder which is, of course, just west of Thayer and then you bird-dogged it. You just pointed your car and drove. In about three or four miles you came to this place.

Well, I'll tell you something about these people. They were unique. They were just a small, little group in sort of, you know, isolation there with hardly any contact with the outside world. But five generations ago, they all got together in a little meeting house and decided that they would be vegetarians. And after that they ate things like tempe scapini and various kinds of tofu, they put it in everything. They also sauteed milkweed florets and then baked them in the oven with a little cream and paprika and grated cheese on them and ate them. They even made oatmeal with orange juice. They said it was very good. Tasty.

So, they ate vegetables. But, you know, it's a little like people with high blood pressure, they'll get on a good medicine that will take care of the pressure and they'll be getting along beautifully and then a year slips by and they just happen to go to the doctor and discover their white blood count is down by half. So they have to get off that medicine, try something else. What I'm saying is, a side effect will suddenly crop up when it's not expected at all or predicted or anything.

Yes. Well, these people had been vegetarians for five generations and suddenly this one particular spring the side effects came upon them. They all began to sprout leaves, they all came out in leaf. You know it was a terrible thing. Dim happened to—this is how Dim got into the story, he happened to be on his way over there because he had an old fourth cousin that he hadn't seen in many years and decided to go over and pay her a visit. She was a lovely old lady who doted on parakeets, she had many parakeets in the house. They used to sit on her shoulders and they would take little seeds out of her mouth and they would speak to her. They would say things like, "How are you today, Mabel?" the sort of thing budgies do. But this doesn't have much to do with the story.

As I say, Dim drove over to see this lovely woman, but she wasn't coming out for anything because she was like all the other old people in I-don't-know-where-it-is. She was afraid to come out because of the woodpeckers. And, you know, everybody had to wear very finely meshed hair nets to keep out the elm leaf beetles. It was terrible to have to comb them out of your leaves. Then there were the little girls and boys. Daisies sprouted from their ears, they were bothered with bees a lot. But they weren't as badly off as the people who went into peach blossoms and had to dodge the hummingbirds. Anyway, here was the whole population growing flowers and weeds. It was all right inside the town but if any of them wanted to shop in Springfield or Carlinville, they were too embarrassed to go.

As I have remarked, Dim came over at that time and he couldn't believe how pitiful everyone was. People around there—why, some outside wag recited "Trees" and they almost killed him. This business of a nest of robins in your hair, you know, you had to take a thing like that pretty seriously if you had a head full of leaves. They admitted that only God could make a tree, but they didn't want any part of the forest.

Where was I? Oh, yes. Dim came into town to see

Mabel Dim, her name was Mabel Dim, that was his cousin's name. Anyway, he saw all these poor people and when the wind blew, all the heads would toss here and there and the blossoms would fall to the ground and have to be swept up.

Well, do you know what Dim had in back of his car? He had two cartons of liver extract. He had gotten them as a small gift from the Sertoma Club for a lecture he had given on the wild turkeys of Illinois. You can guess what happened. When Dim saw everybody in leaf and realized that nobody in the town had eaten any meat at all for five generations, he broke out the liver extract. People lined up and took it by the tablespoonful, they had a yearning for it. It was something like Eskimos wanting whale blubber.

After that it wasn't but two or three days before the leaves began to wilt and when the first good wind came, it cleaned everybody off. And since that day no one has come down with any twiggy illnesses in I-don't-know-where-it-is. Oh, they eat a bit of shaved beef or a little fish once in awhile now, as a diet supplement, kind of a "dimming" at dinner, as they call it, but no one eats any raw meat to this day. They were lucky Dim got there when he did because some of the old people were beginning to put down roots.

Dim excavates his well

You know the story about how Dim found a sunken place in the backyard? It was a round depression about five feet in diameter. So Dim got a hoe and he began to—he was puzzled by that, he began to fool around on the rim of the circle there. Right away he uncovered some homemade bricks, those clayey orange kind, and a light went on in his head. Was this the old well? Dim became excited, he was the kind of fellow who would have been an archaeologist if he had had his druthers. He wanted to dig the well out, see what was there. Well, he knew it was full of clinkers, he was pretty sure of that. People filled their wells up with ashes. The old wells were handy places whenever people cleaned out the old basement furnaces they burned coal in, that Illinois soft coal. But Dim was undaunted, he began to dig out his well. Of course, he had to haul the stuff away himself, he couldn't set it out for the garbage men.

People in the neighborhood talked about Dim's excavation wherever they drank their coffee in the mornings. They thought Dim was foolish, digging out his well. Some were amused because it would have been much cheaper just to get a big pile driver and make a new well. He would have hit water at about 14 feet, they said. But Dim wasn't interested, he had all the water he wanted. What he wanted was to see whether there were some old bottles or buttons, who knows? down in that trash. But mostly the trash was clinkers. Everybody smiled, seeing Dim getting up a sweat on hot days when he should have been on his porch drinking lemonade.

Then in late summer he finally got down to the bottom of the well. He was 20 feet down there and the word went around. It turned out that there was a bunch of rocks down there. Everybody laughed, "Hahaha, he went to the bottom of the well and he came to rocks." But Dim was down there with a flashlight, working away, getting the rocks hauled out, pail after pail, until after a while he uncovered the rim of some kind of a keg. Everybody said, "He's found a barrel of some kind down there." So two men went down to help him out and with some effort they managed to raise the barrel to the top of the well.

Now this wasn't a commercial barrel, it was the kind of barrel the itinerate carpenters used to make for the farmers in winter. They'd come along to the farm and say, "How many barrels you going to need this year?" and the farmer would calculate and they would stay there, work in the barn, and get all the things set up. All the farmer had to do was knock the barrels together, the hoops and the staves and everything. They had no bungholes, they were big barrels to pack apples in.

So that's what Dim found. It took a couple of lines to haul it up. There was nothing printed on it, it was just a big old barrel. He got his crowbar and worked the top off. And you know what was in the barrel? Just more rocks, the barrel was full of chat. And everybody said, "Look at that dumb Dim, he's labored all spring and most of the summer for a barrel full of gravel, hahaha." But Dim didn't pay any attention. He wanted to know what was beneath the gravel, so he scooped the pebbles out by the handful.

And do you know what? Deep down in the gravel he uncovered a six-plank pine box, it was painted a light blue the way they used to paint them. And everybody said, "Look, he's uncovered a six-plank pine box." Well, it wasn't so bad, the box was secured with a hasp and shackle. All he had to do was tap out the oak peg to open the box, tap that out with a hammer. Then he opened the box and it was full of wood shavings, cedar, it smelled delicate, you know, but everybody said, "Oh, well, he's got a box full of cedar shavings. Maybe he can use the shavings to get rid of buffalo beetles and moths hahaha."

But Dim put his hand straight down into the shavings and pulled up an earthenware jug. Everybody's eyes lit up when they read the words on the jug. It said, "MONGA-HELA." Well, there were people standing around there who knew that "Mongahela" was Irish sipping whiskey, the kind they made before moonshiners began to adulterate it. A barrel of that on a steamboat bound from the Golden Triangle of Pittsburgh to New Orleans made for a quick trip, so people were looking at the jug with their tongues out, they were licking their lips. There was a date on the jug, it said "1836." "Mongahela, 1836." It didn't say "MONONGAHELA", it said "MONGAHELA," so they knew it was authentic. It must have been brought to Dim's farm by the original settlers.

Well, people brought their cups and shot glasses over and Dim uncorked the jug, but you know, the whiskey was so thick no one would dare drink it, it made them sick to look at it. Over the years that Mongahela had suffered some kind of a chemical change. It poured like pancake syrup that had been left in the refrigerator too long, so everybody laughed again. They said, "Hahaha, look what Dim has come to. He's got this stomach-rot whiskey that no one would dare touch for all his labor." Dim kept pouring it, though, very patiently, and when no one wanted to offer a cup, he poured it out on the ground. It went glub glub because the air had trouble getting into the jug and everybody stood there grimacing and casting their eyes up to the sky. But when the Mongahela got to the very last glub, the very last, it was so thick it was almost like soft clay dropping out, and just then there was some small object in that last drop that glubbed out and nobody knew what it was. Well, Dim got some gasoline and fished the small object out of the glub and cleaned it off. And it came up shining in his hand, an 1815 one-hundred-dollar gold piece. And everybody shouted, "Oh, oh, he's got an 1815 one-hundred-dollar gold piece!"

Well, you know that coin was worth about $50,000 and everybody said, "Maybe we ought to dig up our wells." They had a lottery fever of sorts, but the wives wouldn't hear of the men digging up the petunias, so their fever was damped out pretty quickly. As for Dim he took the $50,000 and he did things that he wanted to do, he took trips and had the roof repaired.

But he did something else, also. He had the well built up again to its former height, with a housing and a bucket and a handle. A winch and everything, it was very rustic. Of course, the well wasn't open all the way down because Dim didn't want children trying to see to the bottom and falling in. He put an iron grate about three feet below the mouth of the well. He also put a concrete floor in the well, which was dry, you know. There was no water in it and I guess that was why it was filled up with ashes in the first place. Then he had a tunnel built from his basement to the bottom of the well and he put an old bathtub in there that he kept filled with water. And you know what happened? The lovers would come and make wishes and they liked it when they heard the coins hit the water. And fathers would come with their children, and mothers, and they would drop pennies in and the lovers would throw in quarters and people who wanted to put curses on their relatives would throw coins down there also.

So, it wasn't a bad thing for Dim. He made about $15 or $20 a month from the well, just lifting the coins from the tub with a net he kept there and vacuuming the others up that were scattered on the concrete. It kept him in pocket money, he could always go up and get coffee with the old-timers with the well money. He didn't have to dip into his principal, so to speak, and that's the story of how Dim excavated his well.

The mouse henge

This story is kind of poetical. Dim liked to wander around
at night. He was a restless sleeper. One time he got up, it
must have been deep dark just before sunrise. Well, I'll tell
you, you've seen these mushroom rings on the ground in
summer, they call them fairy rings. Well, Dim discovered
what those were. He saw a group of field mice come into
one of those rings just at sunrise. And a mouse who was
obviously a shaman or medicine mouse got in the dead
center of that ring and he sighted the sun coming up over
the horizon, the first rays between two of the mushrooms
that were close together, so that the sun seemed to be
trapped there, if only for a few moments. And that's how
the mice knew when it was the solstice, so the mushroom
rings, as Dim said later, are really mouse henges.
    After that experience Dim always searched for these
mushroom rings when he was out at night. And one night
an extraordinary thing happened. It was about three in the
morning and Dim saw this little procession. And it was
fireflies—the procession was probably two, three feet long,
you know, and that was a procession of mice—and the
fireflies were hovering on the shoulders of these little mice
as they marched through the grass along their little mouse

trails. At the end of the procession there were six mice bearing a litter and on this was the mouse king. He had died, see, and there he was. He was just stretched out there and he had a little silver crown on his head. And as they bore this litter, they were kind of squeaking. Dim guessed that was their equivalent of funeral music. And they went right into the center of one of the mushroom rings. They clawed out a little hole and put the mouse king in there and covered him up. You wouldn't really know it, Dim said, except that a little mound was there that hadn't been there before. So Dim was probably the only man on this earth that witnessed the funeral of a mouse king. It was a lovely story.

The master thief

Dim was in Springfield and, you know, he was not what
you would call a drinker. He didn't like the taste of bour-
bon or scotch very much, but every once in a while he
liked to splash a little booze in the bottom of a tumbler and
put some ice in it and fill it up with water. Make himself a
drink that had a little flavor, it wasn't quite water. So he
stopped in this bar downtown in Springfield, it was somewhere close to the Old Capitol. Anyway, he sat down and
he had this drink. You know, he had to explain to the
bartender what he wanted and the bartender made it for
him for nothing.

So he was—it was, oh, late in the afternoon and he
was feeling pretty good and there was a fellow two bar
stools over, who looked like an old man down in the
mouth. Dim was sympathetic, you know, so he said,
"What's the matter, old-timer, isn't life treating you very
well?"

And this man looked up over his drink and said, "No, it
isn't that. I'm just grieving because of the bad things I've
done in my life."

Dim said, "Everybody has pangs."

And the fellow said, "But mine are like needles or swords. Because when I was a boy I had these itchy fingers. I had this compulsion to steal and my mother would rap my knuckles until they were raw, but she couldn't break my habit."

Well, Dim went, you know, "Tisk, tisk." Like that.

This fellow said, "I would pass the corner newsstand and just going by, all the coins would be swept off the headlines. The paper boys wouldn't even know they were gone. And sometimes I was just mean. There was the time a woman who was poor and had a large family and she had all of her stuff up on the counter of the grocery—that was before the days of shopping carts. And there was a can of Dutch Cleanser and this woman was looking forward to going home and scouring out the sink and cleaning up the toilet and having a nice clean bathtub, and I went by there and just took it. That woman probably went home thinking she had that cleanser and when she went to clean up everything on Saturday, it wasn't there."

Dim was so interested that this fellow continued. Well, I won't tell you all of the details about the criminal activities of this man. He told Dim his name was Thomas Swift and he told Dim about one of his more interesting thefts that occurred at a large party in a big house in Springfield. How he went up the drainspout and into an upstairs bedroom window and took a beautiful emerald necklace from a bureau drawer and how he unscrewed the sash box in one of the bedroom windows and dropped the necklace there into the sash box hole and then screwed the cover back on. And years later when that house came up for sale, how he took a loan and bought the house and then went up and retrieved the necklace and made a big profit.

Dim, feeling uncomfortable, said, "You did stop the thieving, didn't you?"

And the man said that he had.

Well, it turned out that Swift was still living in the mansion and he began complaining about the cost of heat and everything going up and how he was beginning to lose his shirt. And at this point Dim became exasperated.

He said, "You're sitting here telling me that you're sorry for the life you led and you're living off the fruits of your thieving." Dim told him, "You've got to give that all up or you're just dishonest." Dim lectured him sternly like that.

The man burst into tears and he said, "Oh, you're right, you're right."

Then the bartender came up and said, "Tom, you want another drink?"

And Swift said, "No, no, I'm finished for the afternoon." And he reached into his pocket and drew out his wallet but when he opened it, there was no money in the wallet. He was chagrined and embarrassed and stammering and he didn't know what to do and the bartender was standing waiting for the money. So Dim said, "Look, I'll take care of the bill."

It cost Dim 10 bucks. But then it turned out that Swift had a job offer in Chester and he had to be there tomorrow, so Dim added another 30 bucks to get him bus fare to Chester.

And Swift, he was totally grateful. He said, "Well, what should I do? Give me your address and I'll send you the money."

Dim gave him his address, but he said, "Look, don't worry about the money. When you get down to Chester, put what I gave you into a church poor box, and in that way the money will go twice as far."

Well, this man, he was—he just had tears in his eyes and he grabbed Dim and gave him this wonderful, affectionate hug before he left.

And after he left, the bartender came over to Dim and he said, "You don't really think that he's going to put that money in the poor box?"

Dim was surprised and said, "I thought you knew him. You called him Tom."

"Well," the bartender said, "I heard him tell you his name was Thomas."

Dim left the bar then and went home. (Curiously, he notes it was that very day he lost his watch and wallet and he never did know what happened to them. That was a kind of sad day for Dim.) But you know, it wasn't a week and a half later he got a postcard from T.S. and it said that he was still grateful and that he had put the money in the poor box, the 40 bucks. But evidently he didn't do that in Chester because the postcard was from New Mexico, it showed a picture of the old market square in Albuquerque.

The skull of Tola Adams

This story begins in late October. Dim thought he would take a drive to Kampsville, see the hardwoods in their reds and yellows, ride the ferry across the Illinois River and then spend the day puttering in the town, browsing the museum, having some lunch. Which he did. And then he decided to drive north along the bluffs. He did this until he came to a place where he noticed a hole in the limestone where a big oak had slipped down, carrying its root dirt along with it. Dim thought, "Oh, a cave." So he stopped his car and fished a flashlight from the glove compartment. Then he went to the cave, the total darkness of the cave.

But when he entered, he heard a strange sound that made his skin creep, aaaaaaaaaooooooooooowwwwww. That noise would have scared a lesser man, but Dim was intrepid. He marched straight in, flashing his light all around, long ribbons of light here and there in the cave. And the strange sound, aaaaaaaaaooooooooooowwwwww, seemed to be drawing him back to the very end of the cave. Of course, caves have many ends and Dim was in just one of them, a little cul-de-sac. He spotted his light along a ledge and there was a skull gaping back at him—a skull sitting up on its jawbone, with all its teeth and those vacant sockets where the eyes used to be. Dim almost lost his nerve then because that sound, aaaaaaaaoooooooowwwww, moaned right out of the skull. Or it seemed to. Well, caves are usually cool, but the coolness around Dim was dank and it made the skin clammy, like thoughts of mortality.

Dim went up close to the ledge and discovered there was a crack in the wall behind the skull. The wind was coming though the crack and that explained the strange noise, he thought. And then, behind the skull, Dim found a book. He took it and blew the dust off of it and opened it. There was a poem on the first page:

this book of Holy Writ
was all my Scripture
and I Tola Adams
was ever its preacher

Right below the poem was a scrawled note which said, "Will the man who finds this book return it to the above Tola Adams, its owner." Well, Tola is a curious name, but Dim who had read some of the Scriptures himself knew that Tola was the name of one of the judges of Israel, one mentioned in the first book of Samuel. Dim figured that the skull and the book must be related, so he got a box and put them both in it and drove home.

He stored the box in his attic for safe keeping and just like everybody else got busy at all kinds of things, so nothing much happened until Christmas. Dim had a day or two off then, so he took the skull to the state museum in Springfield and showed it to an anthropologist. The anthropologist guessed that the skull belonged to a male Caucasian, perhaps about 29 years old, maybe from the early 1800's. He was impressed by the teeth, an amazingly good set of teeth, hardly a cavity. So Dim went home and enjoyed the colored lights in the windows of his neighbors' houses, and once again got busy doing other things.

Soon it was Valentine's Day, before Dim knew it, that time of year when people have affectionate thoughts about their wives and husbands and everybody is a sweetheart for an evening. Well, Dim was reading a county history, and as he says, his eyes lit on the text and glued there. Because right in that text was the story of Tola Adams. It said that he was a preacher, but not an ordained minister, just someone who read the Scriptures and was anxious to tell everybody what he had learned. He had gone to preach in Kampsville and some river pirates murdered him. They cut off his head and took his clothes and everything and threw the body in a ditch just south of the town.

Fortunately for this story, a neighbor from the village where Tola lived had driven hogs down to Venice for sale in the St. Louis market and he was coming back by way of Kampsville to buy some pearl buttons for his wife because there was a button-making factory there from the mussels they hooked off the shoals in the river. This neighbor was a compassionate man and when he found the body and realized that it was Tola, he tied it to one of his mules and brought it back to the village for burial.

You might want to know how the neighbor recognized the body, it not having a head. It was because of the tattoo. There was a tattoo on the left forearm which said, "Tola loves Hatshepsut." Now the neighbor was pretty certain there couldn't be two such names anywhere else in the county so he carried the body home.

But Dim was beginning to worry about his income taxes and it was mid-April before he got out from under that. Then, when the redbuds were out, he thought a long time and said to himself, "I'll call the reference desk at the Lincoln Library and find out if they know anything about Hatshepsut."

Well, the reference librarian was brimming with information. "Why, yes," she said, "Hatshepsut was queen of Egypt in 1492. It's easy to remember the date. You just have to keep in mind that it was B.C. 1492 and not the more familiar A.D. 1492."

Dim was about to thank her when she went on.

"But you know, she wasn't really queen of Egypt, she was pharaoh. See, the pharaoh wore a ceremonial beard, he just strapped it on his face. So all Hatshepsut had to do to be pharaoh was to put on this beard, which she did, and ruled Egypt. But this outraged a good many men, chauvinistic types. So when Hatshepsut died, her half brother, Phoumas the Third, ordered all the beards broken off of her statues, and you know, they've been that way from that day to this."

Dim was amazed. The librarian had left him breathless and puzzled. Now he knew at least who Hatshepsut was. And he had the skull of Tola Adams. So what else was there to do? Where did he go from here?

Then on the Fourth of July Dim drove over to a small town outside of Carlinville and a little to the east. He liked to visit one or another of the little towns on the Fourth, Nilwood or Womac or Standard City or whatever, and especially towns that had senior citizens selling cake and ice cream. He liked yellow layer cake doubled up with light brown chocolate icing and he liked that with a gob of soft vanilla slathered up against it. A heavenly thought for Dim. But anyway, while he was in that town east of Carlinville he read in the local paper about the pioneer cemetery, which was going to have to be moved because the state was widening the county road and putting in a new bridge. A number of graves were going to be taken up and the remains reinterred somewhere else. Dim was inspired. He knew that the body of Tola Adams was buried in that cemetery.

Nothing happened, though, until the Labor Day weekend, except that Dim had a long conversation with the town fathers and the custodians of the cemetery. So he was there when the people with the spades drove them into the ground and ultimately recovered a lead casket and drew it up to the surface. Well, at this point people were looking here and there and at one another, nobody wanting to desecrate a grave, especially a preacher's. On the other hand, they all knew that Dim had a skull that was probably the skull of Tola Adams, and what more generous thing was there to be done than to return the head to the bones?

So then the mayor looked at the gravediggers and said, "Open it up, boys."

And they broke the seals on the lead casket and threw the lid back. For an instant everyone was stunned. The casket had been airtight and they saw the body exactly as it had been buried. Then the air touched it and it crumbled to dust. No one said a word until Dim, anxious to say anything, said foolishly, "How could he have been in love with an Egyptian queen?"

Now there was an old, white-haired woman who was the town historian and she looked at Dim and said, "Oh, it wasn't that Hatshepsut, it was Hatshepsut Murtock that Tola was married to. The whole town knew about Tola's tattoo. Hatshepsut's mother was a Finney and *her* mother was a Craddock." She went on like that for several more generations. "And you know," she said, "those Murtocks had a lot of money because they invested in bonds to help finance the War of 1812 and also the Erie Canal, which was in 1825. That's how Hatshepsut could afford the lead coffin." The old woman scratched her chin and thought a while. "Yes, there was some gossip about her," she continued, "that she used peroxide on her beard, but that was just malicious talk. It's no wonder after she saw Tola buried that she left town and settled in Quincy. She came back the first year on the anniversary. And then she was heard of in Westport— old Kansas City—and she was the first Murtock to see the Grand Tetons. Some people say there was a mountain named for her, but I don't know whether that's true or not."

Dim brought out his box and he put the skull in the casket, along with a few bits of vertebrae he had found with the skull. Neck bones. He put the book in the casket, too, so that it was returned to its owner. The townspeople felt pretty good about that when they closed the coffin and bound it tight with fence wire and took it over to where there were some nice old cedars and reinterred it. They insisted that Dim stay for the Labor Day picnic. And he did. He enjoyed the polka dances. And he liked the little lanterns that were all colors, the same kind they decorate trailers with during the summer. They were strung up around the park.

The story should end here, but later on in the fall Dim was on a lonesome road driving faster than he should have. It was the time of year when kids are wearing fox masks and appearing as skeletons and tramps and doing their trick or treating. But Dim was thinking that those river pirates must have been frightened when they opened Tola's book and saw that it was the Scriptures. They must have left Tola's head and his book in the cave and gotten away as fast as they could. He was thinking about this when he hit a curve that was too sharp and did a 360-degree skid and dropped 10 feet into a ditch and knocked himself out.

When he came to, Dim could smell gasoline and he remembers saying to himself, "Oh, I'm going to be burnt to death." Well, he lost consciousness again. The flames and smoke were swirling all around and he had this sense of an overpowering dreadful smell of burning bubbling rubber from the tires. He knew the car was going to explode and he was going to be blown to kingdom come. He passed out again, but he must have woken up immediately because he was surrounded by this clammy cool sensation and this gaunt figure, all in black with a hood, was dragging him from the car. And as his own eyes rolled up, he stared directly into the eyes of this figure, sunken back in their sockets. It was as if he were looking a thousand miles and at the end of that thousand miles there were two candle flames burning with such stillness, as if they had never had a breeze to make them flicker. But Dim lost consciousness again.

When he came to the next time, he couldn't figure out what was happening because there was a red light flashing over his head, on and off. Well, that was the light of a police car and there were people gathered around him and he heard this young girl telling the officer, "Why, when I saw him lying there, he looked so peaceful, I thought he was dead."

Dim thought to himself, "Why, that's a strange thing to say. She must be a mortician's girlfriend to say a thing like that."

The highway patrolman smiled at him. "You were lucky, Mr. Dim. If we had gotten here five minutes later, you would have been gone. As it was, you had no pulse and we had to work on you to get you started again."

Dim said, "How did you know I was here?"

"We had a call from the dispatcher and he repeated a message," the patrolman said. "Let's see, how did it go?

come in a hurry
come on the run
come to six-mile and mason
or Dim will be done

So we did that and we found you. You were fortunate, you know, being thrown from the car."

Dim looked into the ditch. All he saw was a mass of broken steel and smoke and fitful flames. And that really knocked him out. He woke up the next morning in a hospital bed, shaken but not hurt at all. So this is the end of a long story. Dim used to say to his friends, it was as near as he ever got to the grateful dead.

Dim and the UFO

This is a rather unusual account, but you have to know that in the fall, in September and October, when the farmers are getting the harvest in, they have to hurry, you know, because it might rain and wet the corn and soybeans and then they'd have to pay to have that all dried out at the elevators, and so they get out in the fields and run their combines all night long. Well, on these murky warm fall evenings if you drive the county roads, the air will be full of dust and there will be these strange lights beetling out in the fields. This is the time of year when the state police get hundreds of calls reporting unidentified flying objects. And of course, well, as I have already explained, what people really are seeing is the farmers getting the harvest in.

But this is what happened one night when Dim was over on the east bank of Sugar Creek. He was interested in that area because he knew that in the early history of the town there used to be Indians would come and hunt on the east bank in the fall. Delaware maybe or Potawatomi or even Kickapoo. He didn't know, he was just over there looking around for arrowheads. It was going on evening and he was out later than he should have been. Well, he was standing in a field entirely by himself when this thing descended from the sky. It was a real UFO. But it wasn't, as Dim reported—well, now, actually he didn't report this aloud because it was such a fantastic story that he was afraid no one would believe him—but he did write it down in a notebook that I bought at a garage sale in Zenobia over on Route 104 near Tovey. I have mentioned the garage and the journal in another story. That's where I found out about the UFO. Well, this wasn't a saucer, it was not like some B-type television UFO. It looked a little more like the kind of machine we landed on the moon in the sixties. Wasn't that in the late sixties? Yes.

Anyway, it landed on these four long legs and stood there kind of peering through the dark and then the bottom of it opened and a sort of lift came down and it was crowded with these alien type creatures, small purple men. They looked, as Dim said, a little like Shriners packed in an elevator at a convention in one of those motels in Decatur. But these small purple men were not smiling and Dim was just stunned watching them as they all stepped off the lift in a kind of knot, you know, and each one of them was carrying an object in his hand, or claw. The objects looked a little like sausages. But then one of the purple men came forward and annihilated a weed. He didn't make a flash of light or anything, he just aimed the sausage at the weed and the weed went up in a puff of smoke. Evidently these aliens thought the weed was standing there aggressively or something.

Well, Dim you know was at his wit's end, so he said, "How are you doing?"

And the leader of the group came up to him—he looked just like the others, but he was the one who came forward and Dim figured he was the leader. And he said, as if he had a slice of ham clenched between his teeth, "We do very well and we have a message."

And Dim said, "Oh, what is it?"

And the leader said, "As we have now sleeted the first leg of our journey from the galaxy Morrisatunia, we will annihilate mankind and all other kind from this planet earth and we will abide here a thousand years before removing once again to Morrisatunia."

Dim thought about the weed and he had a terrible

vision of all humanity destroyed in the world and he said, "Oh, but this is not the planet you are seeking. This is Illinois. Earth is the next planet over."

And the leader and the whole knot of aliens fell back, as if Dim had turned one of those sausages on them. Then the leader said, "Oh, oh, this is embarrassing. We certainly honk you for having expressed us from being called stupid. Oh, oh, we will go up and find this other planet. Meantime, peace and joy to you and have a nice day." And they all waved their claws and got on the lift and went up into the UFO and flew off.

Those aliens never came back. Dim figured that what happened to them was they had been so foolish believing him without checking their star charts that the authorities in Morrisatunia probably called them home to prevent them from making some horrible space blunder. Well, as I said before, Dim never did tell anyone about the UFO, but he had the satisfaction of knowing how he had saved all humankind, even all earth kind, from a sure destruction. Still, there was a fly in his ointment. It was the only time in his life that he told a deliberate falsehood, and he felt bad about that. He was never quite easy in himself for having done that.

Revelations Dim and the great hunt

This story isn't about Dim proper, it's about his great great great grandfather Revelations Dim. This came down through the family and Dim transcribed it faithfully in his notebook. Revelations didn't leave much of a mark legally, you don't find him in the accounts of the first pioneers. But actually he walked into the state. He didn't ride, he just walked. And the family tradition is that he was a great hunter and Dim was proud of that, though he himself did not hunt. So he recorded this exploit of his great great great grandfather Revelations.

You'll remember when the settlers first came, much of this place was prairie. Right through here and all the way down past 104 was all what they called the Springfield Prairie and that merged into the Grand Prairie. It was full of prairie plants and animals and there were timbers, lots of trees along the creeks, and it's a fact that where the governor's mansion now stands there used to a be a place where prairie chickens roosted. Dim only gives this as background.

Revelations was up in this general area one morning and he was a dead shot. But on this particular day when he took aim at a buffalo, the musketball glanced off the tip of the animal's horn. Well, you ask how it was, a dead shot shooting so poorly? The reason was because at the moment Revelations pulled the trigger of his flintlock, he realized he had his foot on a rattesnake.

Now at this point this is a very difficult story to tell. Dim's account is smeared with eraser marks and filled with all kinds of uncertainties. You have to imagine it in slow motion, a kind of stop-frame action. The rattlesnake was reacting to the fact that Revelations Dim had his foot on him. So that was happening just as the buffalo felt this ping on the tip of his horn and took off west at a gallop, while the ball ricocheted in an arc and struck a red fox right between the ears. You see, the fox was sitting there on the edge of a swamp where there were ducks and this fox was saying to himself, "The ducks are on the pond." He was a kind of Abner Doubleday fox.

While this was happening, the buffalo bruised his way across the prairie, dislodging four rabbits who went bounding to the north. They ran over a skunk, who was furious. Of course the rabbits were already gone before the skunk could get his tail up, but what does a skunk know? Meanwhile, the rattlesnake had just gotten himself out from under Revelations' foot. And the fox, who was beginning to react to the ball that had hit him between the ears, vaulted into the sky. But the skunk rushed into a thicket where a panther was studying a mouse. The panther took one look at the skunk with his tail raised and leapt high into a tree. Well, the musketball bounced off the fox's head and carried into another arc, landing in the midst of the ducks in the swamp. And one of the ducks was looking up with its mouth open.

At that point the panther lunged through several trees and suddenly descended onto the back of a black bear, who snarled horribly and charged. The bear didn't know what he was charging at, he just charged. So at one and the same moment the fox was at the top of his astonished leap and the duck was clamping his bill tight on the lead pellet and the bear was charging through the prairie, scaring the willies out of 400 white-tailed deer who were grazing on the other side of the timber. Just then the fox was seen by the ducks and they all flew up at once, 600 of them, startled. They didn't have time to make any altitude so they just flew low toward Revelations and the deer came thundering down on him, also. But, fortunately, right in front of Revelations was a big rock.

So there was the rattlesnake trying to strike Revelations up the side of his head and the ducks beating with their wings just above him and the deer parting right and left of the rock in a storm of hoofs and dust when all at once out of nowhere—dashing in between Revelations and the rock, probably frightened by all the commotion—came this prairie chicken. The prairie chicken did a dance, it ran around in crazy circles.

By that time the rattlesnake had skimmed the side of Revelations' head, miscalculating in all the confusion and nudging a duck in the air but not stunning it with venom, just hitting it. The duck, totally surprised, dropped the musketball. The rattlesnake fell over the antlers of a deer and was carried some 30 yards and dropped into a bank of butterfly weed. Well, as the ducks flew off and the deer bounded away, the ball landed at the foot of the prairie chicken. The bird stopped short, stared at it and fell over dead of a heart attack.

Revelations gave thanks because he had secured his supper without wasting a shot. Then he picked up the chicken and the musketball and went home. His wife Abigail wanted to know how the hunt turned out. Revelations told her it had been "right entertaining."

The heavy hogs

You may have read over Thanksgiving that the domestic turkeys are so heavy these days that the gobblers are unable to mate anymore. Well, a similar thing happened out here and Dim had a part in it, but it concerned hogs. It seems like there was a pig farmer up near Loami and he had heard about Dim's success with the sheep fodder. So he asked Dim if he might be able to prescribe something to put in the hog brew, you know, which Dim did. Now I'm not going to tell what he made because he never specified, but it was done with simple enough swill, just from around the area. Anyway, the farmer fed this to his hogs and the result was the male hogs got so heavy in the haunch, they were unable to get up and mate.

So the farmer called Dim in despair and Dim said, "Well, there's no problem. We'll just rig a winch on a jeep, see, and when you have to mate a hog, you just put this halter on one of the boars and raise him up." Which the farmer did and it was all right, but there was an unexpected result. The hogs associated this with, you know, some simple hog-like pleasure, and it got so any time somebody drove up to the farm or somebody got out of a car and came over to the fence, these hogs would all be over there waiting for the winch, purring like big cats. They became so domestic, they weren't like good Illinois hogs anymore at all. It got so they wouldn't eat in the same trough with the other hogs. They'd just stand over by the fence. But that worked itself out all right because when they stopped eating, they lost all their heavy weight and the first thing you know they turned into cantankerous Illinois hogs again. So, as Dim said, "It's an ill wind that doesn't blow somebody good," which all the pig farmers thought was a pretty fine proverb.

Andy Softlight's
after-shave lotion

This reminds me of a town called Obadiah, Illinois. Have you ever heard of it? Well, it's like any number of towns that no longer exist. The reason Obadiah no longer exists is a fanciful story. There was a cousin of Dim's over there. Now you have to understand there weren't any Dims living in Obadiah, the cousin was by the female relatives. Those were the Softlights that lived over there and one of these was an inventive man by the name of Andy Softlight. Obadiah was a small town, you know, maybe a hundred people. Of the hundred people, a great many were women and children, so maybe we are only talking about 30 men. Right? Enough to enjoy watching a haircut together on Saturday.

Well, anyway, Andy Softlight invented this after-shave lotion you pat on your face, yes, and Dim—really, he has a note that he didn't like to record all this because it was kind of horrible. Well, Andy concocted the lotion. It came in various flavors like, you know, chocolate-mint or raspberry or peach, and it had some alcohol in it as a drying agent and then there were these strange additions like a drop from this jug or two drops from that crock. The stuff must have been made in Andy's basement. Have I told you what it was called? Oh, it was called Balm of Gilead. It was a wonderful, soothing lotion.

But you know what happened? Well, it's odd about these little towns, they're founded and they rise to expectations and then they fall. Towns are like people and the seasons, there's a kind of cyclical aura about them. That's what Dim said anyway. Winters come and the spring and the summer and the fall and so on.

Well, the fellows in Obadiah put on this after-shave lotion, but it tasted so good they wanted to lick it off all the time. And they would get so that some would lick in clockwise directions and others would go counter clockwise. And that would have been all right, you know. You could do that in front of a mirror and be done with it. But they couldn't stop. And because of some strange ingredient, proteins or something that were in this lotion, their tongues suffered genetic mutations and grew long and narrow and very sticky at the ends, so that a man could swipe up his whole face and get all the lotion off. Of course, there were some there who were absent-minded and they would slurp it up in any old direction.

Well, you know, it was kind of addictive. These men would —they didn't want to do anything but put on this after-shave lotion and lick it off. Then another unexpected thing occurred. They became like lizards, they could shoot out their tongues and catch flies on the wing. Of course, in those days there were a lot more flies than there are now because we have so many pesticides and fly killers. It got so that these men could support themselves in terms of nutrition on just the flies they'd catch and they stopped eating anything else, and working even.

Oh, it caused consternation in the town. Women became huffy because the women didn't shave, you know, so their tongues were just like everybody else's. But there was more to it than that. It got so the little boys would try to imitate their fathers. They would go around jabbing at gnats. Well, that was enough for the grandmothers. Those women took the children because they didn't want them addicted and they left town. And some of the men, they felt the same way and they went away with the women. They had their mothers or their wives put adhesive tape over their mouths so they would not be tempted by flies anymore or want to lick the after-shave lotion off. After a while their tongues returned to normal, but it was painful.

Finally there were only about five men left in that town, everybody else was gone. These were the diehards. And they were sitting around this table in back of the pharmacy, all talking about the business of everybody leaving Obadiah, when a fly circled down and lit right in the middle of that table. And you know there was this long, studied pause and then all of a sudden, at precisely the same moment, they shot their tongues out and hit that fly. Well, the fly was devastated, as you can imagine, but so were the men. All their tongues were stuck there, stuck to the table where the fly had landed.

It was days later, according to Dim, that a consultant for the Illinois Department of Agriculture happened to be going through Obadiah, he wanted to see what was happening to the corn in the area, you know. And he looked in the window of the pharmacy and saw those five men sitting there with their tongues glued to the table. They were all dead. Oh, yes, their hearts must have given out with their tongues, Dim thought. But it was merciful in a way, he said, although he could not think why. You know what they had to do for the funeral? They had to just take them up, table and all, on a plywood platform, with two forklifts. Luckily one of the people who left town had just dug a big hole on the north side of his house for a cesspool and they buried them right there together.

Of course, the town has long since disappeared—nobody wanted to come back to it. Some people came and got lumber and barn siding and it was vandalized, but nothing much else happened to it. Finally it was just bulldozed out of the way. It's really covered up by a cloverleaf over there on I-72, or is it I-74? And some of the people from the town are still living, but the men never dared to shave again. Even if Softlight's lotion was all gone, they were afraid some other lotion might trigger memories. These men were known ever after as "Van Winkles." You can find them sometimes in this or that little town in central Illinois, even today.

The singing dogs

There was an afternoon when Dim decided to play his
harmonica and he was having a good time and he decided
to play, "Have You Ever Been to Meeting, Uncle Joe, Uncle
Joe?" and his dog Sleuth perked up his ears and sang right
along. Dim was amazed. He said, "Sleuth can sing!" Then
he played "On the Cold Coast of Greenland" and Sleuth—
well, Sleuth sang right along with that one too. So Dim
thought about this and then he went out and got five or six
of the more companionable dogs from the neighborhood
and brought them inside his house. Then he played "The
Arkansas Traveler" and all those dogs sang along. Dim
thought, "Why, a troop of singing dogs!" So the rest of the
summer he practiced with them, you know, he would give
them little bits of bologna or a few raisins if they did well.

Finally, it was the Labor Day picnic and Dim thought he
would take them up to the park so they could perform for
the townspeople. Dim had all the dogs on the stage, he
was just ready to begin and they were sitting there. They
were very polite for dogs, you know, they weren't biting
anybody or each other. And Dim was just about to play
"Buffalo Gals" when this ring-tailed cat walked along in
front of the stage. It was an old cat, not one afraid of dogs,

but those seven dogs saw that cat and they took out after it and it went up a tree. Got away.

Well, the townspeople were all amused. They said, "Yeah, Dim and his vanishing dog act, they must be playing `The Lost Chord.'" Barbs like that. And Dim couldn't get the dogs to come back up on the stage, so he just left them and went home. He felt disgraced, but the dogs remained at the picnic and had a wonderful time eating barbecued pork scraps and whatever else they could find on the grounds.

But you know, it wasn't two weeks later Dim was in his house playing "Lead, Kindly Light" on his harmonica and Sleuth began to sing along. You know what Dim did? He took Sleuth out and tied him to a tree in the backyard. He told Sleuth, "Once bitten is twice shy" and went back into the house and finished the song by himself.

Future Dim

Well, there's another story that involves a descendent of Dim's. This is a story about, well, it's a strange story. Actually it was a dream that Dim had. He had worked very hard one day and fell into a sound sleep and dreamed a future dream. This involved a Dim who lived in this society, oh, I suppose not very—in some ways in terms of locality, perhaps where we are now, but in this society they had all these, you know, intelligence machines. You plugged one in and it would match you up with somebody who was compatible, that kind of thing. At a certain time in a fellow's life, in everyone's life in that society, you did that. And Dim found that he was suitable for a woman by the name of LuLulallia Frangepon.

Now you can tell from a name like that that she probably wasn't a true descendent of earth. In fact she came from a remnant group that had flown in from a distant planet years before. The Frangepons were a species of humans, but had been away from earth for so long a time that when they came back, they had claws. As a matter of fact, though, it didn't take them very long to return to the normal human shape, so that they had hands like anyone else, their hands just looked a little arthritic. I should explain that the future Dim's name wasn't really Dim, he was Dimnus 845. The 845 is the number of generations from the Dim we know. It was all from a certain time, what they called "the great changeover."

But about LuLulallia and Dimnus 845, it was not necessarily, you know, a relationship grounded in sex, so much as two people who were sort of naturally companionable. The intelligence machines saw to that. They kind of complemented each other, felt good in each other's presence. But once a relationship such as this was established, then the partners were able to gale. That's what it was called — "galing." In other words, they could combine their talents and come up with, perhaps, a product of some kind, something that could improve the life of the planet. People didn't speak in those future days in terms of anything but the planet. And Dimus did this with the Frangepon girl, LuLulallia. He galed with her.

What she was able to contribute to the relationship, the galing, was anything that was beautiful. She could make any old object beautiful. And what Dimnus was able to contribute was something of interest and use made out of very common things, that was his ability. And what they combined to do was to produce an object about the size of a stick of chewing gum. In fact, when they became entrepreneurs, they packaged it as a little stick of what looked like—they wouldn't know what our gum wrappers were, but that was what they made them look like. And what this stick did, well, it was made out of common cleaning solutions on the part of Dimnus, such as you would find around in the house. But you have to remember that house cleaning at that time was nothing like what we can appreciate. Someone would have an object, you know, in their hand and they would press a button and it would shoot out all these collectrons that would just gloam all around, say, in the kitchen and then when the person pressed the return button, the collectrons would swoop back in with all the dust and everything. Then the dust was dropped into little bins and returned to the reprocessing plant.

But anyway, Dimnus took some of the collectrons and combined them with some chemicals to make what really amounted to a mild explosive and with the Frangepon touch for beauty, they managed to make an attractive little object that could be sold quite cheaply and everyone could enjoy on picnics and whatnot. It went off pretty much like our little flowerpots that we ignite on the Fourth of July, only it would last much longer. And on birthdays and family outings and mild celebrations, this is what people would do, they just would unwrap one and set it to begin and about three or four minutes later, it would make these lovely showers of sparks. Well, they sold like hot cakes, everybody bought them. They must have had some nostalgia in their blood for old timey earth festivals, I guess.

Now here Dim's dream took a bad turn. Those sticks were not as stable as Dimnus and LuLulallia thought because if you didn't use them right away, if you sat one on the shelf, it became more powerful. People began to understand this quickly because once the sticks were marketed, anybody could put one of them in a chemscan and see what it was made out of and could duplicate it. And what they had was Dimnus without Frangepon, a dreadfully useful thing that became hideously more and more powerful.

The authorities couldn't even recall the stuff. Because what would they do with it if they had it all? And for a moment in the history of humankind, everybody had one of these in their shirt pocket and there wasn't anything the government could do. Oh, there would be drives with slogans like, "Get the rocket out of your pocket." But these campaigns were flops, just cosmetic controls, so to speak. Old ladies, for instance, kept sticks in their bras and they wouldn't give them up because they knew no one was going to try to snatch a purse if they thought an old lady might explode on them, don't you see. So, for one instant in the history of humankind nobody was any more powerful or dangerous than anybody else.

There was only one problem. Now this is all reported about Dimnus by Dim—from Dim's dream. You remember it was Dim's because it's all in there in his notebook. One evening one of those sticks did go off and it set another one off about 40 yards away. So suddenly gum sticks began to go off everywhere. They went off all over the world or the planet, as those people called it, and Dim was seeing this in his dream. And nobody knew what was going to happen, until finally there is just a big line that sweeps across the bottom of the page where Dim was writing. And that is all that can be said about this whole thing. Dim woke up, I guess.

Dim's favorite poem

Dim was very literary. Sometimes on a winter evening he, like everyone else, would recite his favorite poem. He would do this in the very deep of winter and in late fall or early spring. All he needed was a good fire in the hearth, swamp oak logs or osage, and then he would be ready to go:

> When the dim day is buried
> Beyond the world's sight,
> low-lingering lurid,
> A sorrowful light
> Is left on the hilltops;
> While bitter winds blow
> Swept down from those chill tops
> And summits of snow.

Dim would get very emotional and theatrical. He would recite the lines in a powerful voice to his dog Sleuth, drowsing in front of the fire, and Sleuth would sometimes lift up an ear:

> The muskrat and mink
> Are all that is left now;

> So nations depart;
> And Nature, bereft now,
> Place yieldeth to Art.

Dim would sound his "Place yieldeth to art" like the Anglican Bishop who had in the margin of his sermon, "Argument weak here. Yell like hell." This would make him feel better and he would go on:

> But the heart no change knoweth:
> The stream shifts its side;
> Wind cometh and goeth,
> But sorrows abide.

Once he got this far, Dim would carry on to the very end:

> Though the wave and the earthquake
> May swallow the shore,
> Yet wild sorrow and heart-break
> Will part nevermore!

Dim always paused between "part" and "nevermore" for the effect. Of course, he only did this when he was alone with Sleuth and the fire in the hearth. He didn't recite if there was company. So, if he had to dry his eyes with a handkerchief once in a while, it was all right.

The Shimer College girls

This goes way back to Dim's youth. When he was a young man, he went up to the northwestern part of the state. You know, that's what they call the Palisades, up there along the Mississippi where there are these huge bluffs. Well, Dim was up there around Savanna and Mount Carroll—remember, old Shimer College was there. But before it was Shimer College, it was what they call a female seminary, girls lived up there in the dormitories. It happened that one of Dim's cousins, Moravia Softlight, was in her second year there.

Now Dim, he was working on the river. He was a wharf boat assistant, he just swept the dirt out and kept an eye on the cats and he had to be there when the boats came in, packet boats in the Mississippi trade. Other than that he had lots of time and he'd go over to the college in the evenings.

Of course, you know in those days at any college it was, what's the Latin phrase? *In loco parentis,* yes, they chaperoned the girls. There was a formidable lady who always stayed down in the front room of the girls' dorm. Nobody got in there after 7:30 at night. But the girls would let this large wicker basket down on a line, see, from the third floor, and then Dim would get in. Well, when you're young—

He'd get in this big basket and they'd haul him up. And they'd have, you know—it was in the days before things went wrong, it was a time of innocence and they would chat and have taffy and divinity fudge. Well, in Champaign-Urbana people were always bad, but everywhere else in the state it was different, so anyway—but even then there were people who had evil minds. And the word kind of spread around Mount Carroll that there was something nefarious going on in the dorms. And one night the town sheriff came out and he heard—somebody reported that what Dim did was, he'd give a little whistle, like a small song sparrow, and then this basket would come down.

Well, this sheriff went out to the college one time when Dim wasn't even there and he did the sparrow whistle and, you know, the girls thought it was Dim and they let the basket down and he got in. Well, Dim was a slight little fellow. He probably weighed, you know, a little bit more than a zucchini when he was young. This sheriff was a big man and he had all his revolvers on and the girls knew it was a heavy basket, but they thought maybe Dim was bringing some friends, so they'd have to get out more divinity fudge and they were excited and getting ready to yell things like "Men on the floor" in case some of their roommates were taking showers.

Well, anyway, they got the basket up almost to the window ledge and one of the girls said, "Oh, oh, it's the sheriff." And they threw up their hands in dismay and down went the—well, fortunately for him he landed in a big springy bush so he didn't break anything, an arm or anything. It would have been embarrassing for the school, except that the sheriff didn't want to press charges because he would have looked like a real ninny, you know, being dropped in a basket like that.

Dim, he kind of got the word, though, so he went back downstate after that and he never went up in the basket in the female seminary dorm again. He thought it would be too chancey. So he had to say goodbye to his cousin Moravia and her lovely friends and the divinity fudge and all. So that's the story of Dim and the basket. Some people may think it's depressing. Well, yes, but that's the way life is, as Dim would say.

Crismouse

One time Dim went into his living room unexpectedly and
there was a mouse eating a bit of cracker someone had
carelessly dropped on the floor. Now the mouse did not
panic and scurry under the sofa. It continued to nibble the
cracker and when the cracker was gone, the mouse
stretched itself to its full height. Then, joining its small
forepaws together, it made a profound bow to Dim.

Well, Dim was amazed and he, in turn, bowed to the
mouse. Now why would he do that? Dim says that he knew
that this was no ordinary mouse. No, it was the Mouse King
come visiting on the 25th of December, as a matter of fact.
And so ever after, Dim always placed three or four oyster
crackers in a blue English castleware saucer for the Crismouse—as Dim always called him, being somewhat sentimental.

And Crismouse appeared beneath Dim's pine tree,
which was decorated with small lights and ornaments,
some of those ornaments survivors of Dim's own ancient
past, and long streamers of red ribbon. The mouse always
came at precisely 18 1/2 minutes after 10 in the morning and
Dim always imagined that Crismouse could never afford to

be a second late because he had to keep abreast of his schedule of important visits and ceremonial events.

Now Dim always pretended that he did not see the mouse nibbling the oyster crackers, he felt that it would be unseemly watching the Mouse King eating. And the mouse for its part never looked at Dim until its mouse brunch was all gone. Only then did the two of them bow to each other. And only then did the Crismouse walk majestically across the rug and disappear behind the wooden chest in the northeast corner of the living room.

Dim mentions a strange thing here. As often as he cleaned behind that chest, sometimes moving it far away from the walls to dust behind it, he never saw an opening in the baseboard where a mouse could enter. Still he knew as certain as taxes that the mouse would be there under the tree at $18^1/2$ minutes after 10 on the 25th of December.

You can imagine what a short fuse Dim had when any of his friends wanted to praise *The Nutcracker Suite*. He said the thing had no plot after the toy soldiers won their cheap victory. But he liked the "Waltz of the Flowers." Crismouse would be happy in a meadow, he thought.

Dim's dream

It was after Christmas, maybe the 29th or 30th, and Dim
went to New Harmony. New Harmony is on the other side
of the Wabash from Phillipstown and Crossville. He had to
go over an old bridge, it cost him a quarter. He was interested in the Rappites, a mystical Lutheran group who
founded New Harmony. They planted a maze, which Dim
took some time to study, because they knew how difficult
it was to live harmoniously with friends and neighbors in
this life. The maze was supposed to illustrate the difficulty,
it was the sort of thing Dim could appreciate.

Then he drove straight north on Indiana 41, picked up
150 on the other side of Vincennes and followed it into
Illinois and Route 16 for Charleston. He wanted to have
lunch in Charleston and look around the town, maybe get
out to the university, see the buildings and the coeds,
although it was just the buildings he was interested in, Dim
says he told himself.

Well, he was driving along not bothering a soul and
getting ready to drop down into the valley of the Embarras
River—Dim especially enjoyed dropping down into river
valleys on days he was out driving—when he almost lost
control of the wheel. Oh, he had caught out of the corner

of his right eye a glimpse of a terrifying hominid striding above the trees, it must have been 40 or 50 feet tall. Dim pulled over to settle his heart. He saw then that the figure was a statue of some kind and there was a side road you could take to drive up to it, so he did.

What he found was a statue of Abraham Lincoln with a head too big for that 40 foot tall body. The thing appeared to be—it looked like it had been made up and just escaped from a burial plot, like it was some Boris Karloff loose in the woods of eastern Illinois. Dim walked around it. Someone had blasted a hole in the back of the left leg, so Dim could see that the statue was made out of some kind of tough plastic molded on a form of slats and chicken wire and there were empty beer cans in the cavity. Well, Dim felt this was in bad taste and went back to his car.

Then he saw that a group of women had driven into the little park. They were sitting in their Chevrolet with their legs out, feet just touching the gravel road, ready to jump back in the car if the thing moved. Even though Dim told them the statue was made out of plastic, they continued to look at it with apprehension and drove away from the place when he did.

Dim was shaken up a little himself, not quite able to define just how he was feeling. He was feeling a little queasy and he didn't want any lunch. But the town was all right. He visited the museum at the university. There were some nice things there, he thought, especially the little basket. It was a little tire-shaped basket woven of natural wool and sea oats, with a handle of grapevine and this with its tendrils still on it. Dim figured the basket had no practical value. It was no good, say, for sewing, a place to put spools of thread and packages of needles, a small scissors and a tape measure. No, any such use would destroy the tendriled handle. The basket was the shape someone from a small eastern Illinois town had brought out of mind.

Dim drove west again after visiting the museum, west into a crimson evening sky, through Decatur and Springfield and on home. He was exhausted, the long trip and all. So he went to bed at 10 and fell asleep like a rock—it seemed for only a minute, but really, it was two in the morning when he awoke. He was inside a dream and he was surrounded by these toads. Plastic toads and imitation plastic toads. Dim couldn't tell which was which. That was the horror of it. Blind, grinning toads. Three in particular were eating all the smaller ones and these smaller ones seemed to want to be eaten. Dim felt the little hairs rising on the backs of his arms above his wrists. These slimy toads. Harsh purples and bilious greens, these toad colors being gulped down. And Dim was staring through the darkness, knowing as these three ate the others that a larger shadowy figure of a toad was looming at the foot of his bed. Its eyes—well, the left one, a diamond button, circled counter clockwise, and the right, a faceted ruby, circled clockwise so that the toad seemed much bigger than it was. Indeed, Dim understood that all the toads in his room seemed bigger than they were. Clunch clunch, that was the sound of the smaller ones being eaten by the larger ones, clunch clunch, followed by a miserable scrinching noise. Dim did not want to think about it.

Then the largest toad ate the last three, the most vicious ones, and Dim dreamed within his dream, dreamed in pain as the largest toad caught his ankle in its mouth and began gumming his foot. Dim dreamed he was walking on a plateau of flint and this sharp metal thing came up behind him and clamped its steel teeth on his shoulder. Dim stiffened and his cry was paralyzed in his throat and now the toad had Dim's leg up to the knee and Dim was suddenly raging with pain and anger, the brute mindlessness of it all.

That was when he heard the voice, one that he knew, but had never heard before. But the words of this voice came apart and hung in the air around him. They were letters, small letters, letters of polished jade assembled into words and phrases—"feeling of sadness" "everything" "children have been born" "ever I may return" "who can go with me" "be well" "prayers" "affectionate"—these were the words hanging in the air around Dim's bed. And then Dim understood what the basket of wool and sea oats and wild grapevine with tendrils, what the basket he was holding in his hands was for. He reached out and took each word, one by one, and placed it in the basket. Then he went downstairs and put the basket on his mantel. You may be wondering about the toad, but there is nothing to wonder about. There was no toad when Dim began to see the words and hold the basket in the deep darkness there.

And when he returned to his room, imagine this, there was a woman standing at the foot of his bed where the toad had squatted. She was dressed in some classical way, as Dim recalled, in a voluminous dress. She looked like the University of Illinois Alma Mater, the Lorado Taft statue on the corner by the student union. And this woman had a scalpel, such as a surgeon might use, and with this she made a small incision in Dim's upper right arm. Dim felt no pain, he just stood there as all the restlessness, the disbelief, the anger oozed out of him.

As he became faint from the blood loss and drifted into his second dream within a dream, he was in a country where the drops of rain danced above the blades of grass and coaxed them up from the ground. Dim was standing in this fertile meadow when suddenly he was overwhelmed. Something enveloped him, some power that had no limit and Dim fell to the ground and tried to bury his head in the grass. It was almost instinctive, he remembered, that he knew he didn't have to be afraid. And then every cell in his body seemed to separate itself from the others and vibrate. At this point Dim had a problem. Should he count 1,000,000,000,000 cells or calculate as well the cells of all the comfortable parasites that shared his body with him? In which case there would have to be maybe 100,000,000,000,000 cells that were vibrating. But no matter. "Oh," Dim wrote, "it was a moment of unspeakable joy. And then it passed."

He knew he could sleep then, ascending through many dreams. Yes, he slept a long time and when he woke, he was far into the day and the coming of the New Year. And he would not have remembered any of these dreams except for the scar on his right arm. He knew that the scar had not been there before. Dim was amazed. He thought he should make some New Year's resolutions.